KAREN McCOMBIE

SUNSHINE, SUNBURN and NOT-SO-SWEET NOTHINGS

■SCHOLASTIC

for Hilary and Ellie

(with lurve and thanx)

Scholastic Children's Books,
Euston House, 24 Eversholt Street
London NW1 1DB, UK
a division of Scholastic Ltd
London ~ New York ~ Toronto ~ Sydney ~ Auckland
Mexico City ~ New Delhi ~ Hong Kong

First published in the UK by Scholastic Ltd, 2006

10 digit ISBN 0 439 95056 2
13 digit ISBN 978 043 995056 5

Printed and bound by Nørhaven Paperback A/S, Denmark

10 9 8 7 6 5 4 3

Papers used by Scholastic Children's Books are made
from wood grown in sustainable forests.

Sunshine, Sunburn and Not-So-Sweet Nothings

Sitting there in the shack-of-a-hut-of-a-loo, with a light breeze drifting through the window and chilling my bum, I reminded myself of the promise I'd made earlier: to have a good time, even if Linn and Rowan didn't plan to. In fact, I decided that whatever happened, I was going to ignore it, rise above it, and not let *anyone*, or *anything* spoil my week!

That profound thought zapped into my head exactly a half a second before Rolf lifted his head and started growling, and a full second before the shack-of-a-hut-of-a-loo door was yanked open and two strange faces stared in at me. . .

To find out more about Karen McCombie,
visit her website www.karenmccombie.com

Contents

PROLOGUE

Dear Grandma,

Hurrah! You've got flu!

I don't mean that in a *horrible* way, in case you just read that and thought "Mmm, Ally is suddenly my *least* favourite grandchild. . ."

I just thought you must be exhausted from our summer holiday, and glad of a rest. Not that you came on holiday *with* us; it's just that being left to feed and look after all of our zillions of pets is a full-time job, and lying in bed with a box of Kleenex, a copy of *Country Living* magazine and Stanley bringing you cups of tea and HobNobs all day must seem like heaven compared to being an unpaid zookeeper.

Oh, by the way, Tor is here (sort of – he's playing hide-and-seek with Ivy and is talking to me in a muffled voice from inside my wardrobe), and he says sorry that the boy mice chose the week we were away to have upset tummies. It can't have been much fun for you, but I guess cleaning up mouse diarrhoea is a lot easier than if our family was unfeasibly posh and rich and asked you to look after a herd of thoroughbred horses (with stomach bugs) while we were away. Phew – thank goodness we're poor!

Um ... call me psychic, but I have a funny feeling you've read this far and have started shaking your head and muttering, "Why does Ally *always* have to ramble so much? Why can't she get to the point?"

Well, the point is, Mum told me recently that you thought it was very sweet that I wrote down all the family sagas and saved them up for her during the four years that she was ... er ... away travelling/missing/not living with us/whatever you want to call it.

("Ally, dear, *please* get on with it!" I'm positive I can hear you sigh.)

Still, *just* in case you get fed-up reading *Country Living* magazine or those lady detective novels I know you like, I thought the following pile of pages might pass the time. It's the saga of our summer holiday, with all its ups, downs, sunburn, silliness, and not-so-sweet nothings.

Hope you like it (and hope all the rambling doesn't do your head in*).

Love you lots,

Ally
(your Grandchild No. 3)

* Speaking of things that will do your head in . . . I don't want to spoil the surprise, but I'd better warn you that Rowan has made you a very sparkly get well card. You might want to open the envelope over the sink, otherwise you'll be hoovering glitter and sequins out of your nice, neat crumb-free carpet for weeks.

ASK A STUPID QUESTION

I opened my mouth to take a crunch of raw carrot, and instead a really stupid question popped out.

"What's up?" I said, suddenly noticing my sister's extra-pinched face.

"Nothing," Linn snapped, in a way that meant "Something, but don't ask, because I'm not going to tell you". So I shut up and crunched on my carrot instead.

Hmmm. The Grouch Queen wasn't a happy bunny.

My eighteen-year-old sister Linn (the Grouch Queen) is never what you might call bright and breezy (tense and tetchy, more like), but this particular teatime, while she was sitting ramrod straight, silently dissecting her veggie sausage, her body language was screaming "AAAAAARRRRGGGHHH!!"

Here were the giveaways: 1) she was gripping her knife so hard that it was practically sawing through the plate, 2) her lips were pressed so tightly together that they'd completely disappeared, 3) her nostrils were flaring same as a Spanish bull's does when it's had enough of the bloke in the spangly jacket trying to throw sharp, pointy sticks at it and decides to see how *he* fancies a horn up his bum instead.

Of course, I knew the *main* thing that was bugging Linn; the results of her A-levels were weeks away, but she'd already started fretting in earnest that she wasn't going to get good enough grades to do her dentistry course in Edinburgh.

Results-fretting aside, what was irritating Linn right at this particular time was . . . well, being related to all of *us*, I guess. The Love family: a jumble of people, large (Mum, Dad, Linn, me and Rowan) and small (Tor and Ivy), variously colourful (Mum and Rowan), dippy (Rowan), messy (me and, er, Rowan) and loud (not Tor, who never bothers speaking very much). Add to that three dogs, five cats and an unfeasible amount of other pets all squashed together in our cluttered, ramshackle, north London house, and sometimes it all gets too much for neat-freak Linn.

So what was our family guilty of doing today? I let my eyes act like a camera, scanning round the table, documenting everything that could possibly be winding Linn up right now.

Well, let's start with the obvious. . .

Name: Rowan.
Age: 16.
Status: Airhead sister.
Currently: Laughing too loudly at something only mildly funny that her boyfriend Alfie had said.

Rowan had been dating Alfie – an indie lovegod and Linn's best mate – for over a year now, and still couldn't believe her luck (hence the adoring looks and over-the-top giggling at His Handsomeness's slightest funny remark). Linn couldn't believe Rowan's luck, *or* Alfie's taste. Normally, she hung out with Alfie separately, but tonight – thanks to Mum inviting him to stay to tea – Linn was forced to watch all the lovey-doveyness of Rowan and Alfie at uncomfortably close quarters, and I think it was giving her heartburn or something.

Moving the camera along, next on Linn's bugged-list was. . .

Name: Tor.
Age: 8.
Status: Animal-obsessed little brother.
Currently: Making a working model of Vesuvius out of mashed potato and *way* too much tomato sauce. (The Pompeii volcano is one of Tor's favourite historical foodie sculptures: others are

toast pyramids and the Eiffel Tower constructed from Cheese String.)

The problem was, to get a vaguely authentic explosion of "lava", Tor was splashing a teaspoon into the tomato gloop, sending speckles of fiery redness far and wide and dangerously close to Linn's white shirt. She'd already asked him to stop, and already asked Mum and Dad to ask him to stop, but Mum and Dad just went "hmmm?" in a distracted way and kept smiling funny little secret smiles at each other. (Our parents being oblivious to Love family chaos was bugging Linn too, I knew.)

Or maybe Mum and Dad just couldn't hear Linn properly, thanks to something (someone) else that was bugging Linn.

Name: Ivy.
Age: 4.
Status: Very cute little sister.
Currently: Making up a song about mud.

Ivy's mud song didn't exactly have a catchy tune (make that *any* tune), but the lyrics were pretty easy to remember, since they consisted of the word "mud" being repeated over and over again.

I didn't suppose it was going to land her a deal

with Sony records any time soon, which was a pity, as she's very photogenic (she looked cute as a particularly cute button in her nursery class photo), has a real gimmicky look (she won't wear anything but pink), and a strong fan base (the dogs were wowed by her singing – or maybe it was just the half-a-veggie-sausage she was wafting about in her hand).

The one-word, no-tune mud song, and the fact that Rolf, Winslet and Ben were snurfling and circling and drooling was doing Linn's head in, for sure. Put it this way, if *I* had three wishes, they'd be 1) world peace, 2) an extra day at the weekend, and 3) an endless supply of free crisps, whereas Linn's would be 1) world peace, 2) non-frizzy hair, and 3) a neat, tidy, quiet and crumb-free family.

"Ivy – do you want to sit down and finish your tea?" I said gently.

I couldn't do much about Rowan mooning and giggling over Alfie, and I wasn't close enough to Tor to nick the spoon from his hand, but maybe I could ease Linn's stress by encouraging Ivy to shut up and eat up.

"Nope!" giggled Ivy, interrupting her mud song for the briefest of seconds to answer my question. "*Mud, mud, MUD!! Mud, mud, MUD!!*"

Well, I tried, I thought to myself, taking a crunch of carrot.

Uh-oh.

I could feel an evil, death-ray glare suddenly boring into the side of my head. Guess who was guilty of bugging the Grouch Queen now?

Name: Ally (i.e. me).
Age: 14.
Status: Love Child number three.
Currently: Working Linn's tattered nerves with my noisy choice of nibbles.

Trying to act casual, I started sucking the rest of my raw carrot, wondering how many days it would take to dissolve, and if I could survive a whole summer of Linn being in top-gear grump mode. . .

"Hey, guys!" said Dad, trying to get all our attention. No one but me, Linn and Mum took any notice of him. (Mum was resting her chin in her hands, half her face hidden behind her fists, her eyes sparkling with whatever secret-something that she and Dad were about to spill.)

"*Guys!*" Dad said in a slightly louder voice.

Rowan and Alfie fell silent, and Tor paused in his efforts to recreate an AD 79 volcano in potato.

"*Mud, mud, MUD!! Mud, mud, MUD!! Mud, mud, MU—*"

Amazing; as soon as I put my hand over her

mouth, Ivy stopped bouncing and froze, and so did all three dogs, as if they were playing some kind of copycat game.

"Guess what?" Dad grinned at us all.

Cue two seconds of no one saying anything, and everyone's minds whirring.

"Ahhh!!" gasped Rowan, slapping her hands to her mouth and making her myriad bangles jangle. "You're going to have another *baby*!!"

I think we all jumped in shock – especially Mum and Dad.

"No, *no*! What made you think *that*?" Dad then laughed.

Rowan looked momentarily deflated, and I felt kind of sorry for her. I mean, "Guess what?" is vague and important-sounding at the same time, isn't it? The answer could have been anything from "Mum and I are opening a spoon shop!" to "We've decided to paint a mural of a double-decker bus on the front of the house!" to "We're going to move you all into a caravan in the garden and rent your rooms to clowns! Won't that be fun?" So in the circumstances, Rowan's baby suggestion didn't seem *too* wild an idea.

Actually, I hoped my parents were going to say something much more dull yet brilliant, like "We're getting a new TV!" Yeah, so we'd all gotten used to watching our favourite programmes in shades of green, but being able to see them in full colour . . . wow. And being able to switch the TV on in the first place without using an on-button that was loosely held in place with Blu-tack would've been *stupendously* exciting.

Please say it's a new TV, please say it's a new TV. . . I muttered in my head.

"Well, it's a lovely surprise," Mum jumped in to explain. "And while it's for everyone, it's especially for Linn – a treat before she goes away to university."

It could STILL be a new TV! I tried to convince myself. After all, a pair of state-of-the-art hair straighteners wouldn't be much of a lovely surprise for the rest of us, unless Tor or Ivy fancied passing a rainy hour giving Rolf and Winslet's scruffy fur a to-die-for, salon-smooth look.

"What sort of surprise?" Linn asked Mum.

My big sister had an unconvincing smile of curiosity plastered on her face, but her eyes had a glaze of pure panic. Linn doesn't like surprises; they're too messy. The week before, she'd just rearranged her nail varnishes alphabetically, by shade name. If you're the sort of person who needs to have "Nearly Nude" come after "Natural Blonde", you really aren't up for any bolt-out-of-the-blue shockers.

"We. . ." said Dad, pausing for dramatic effect, ". . .are going on holiday!! For a whole week!"

"Yay!" yelped four Love children, and a couple of dogs (who didn't know quite what they were yelping at).

I realized it was time to take my hand away from Ivy's mouth, as all her yaying was leaving dribbles on my palm. I also realized that the smile on Linn's face was so frozen that she was at serious risk of contracting hypothermia. Living in the midst of our madhouse was tricky enough for Linn; being stuck with us all day-in, day-out was going to be like a terrible form of torture for her.

"Are we going to Disneyland?" Ivy asked breathlessly, eyes a-glow with happy possibilities.

"Um, no . . . we're going to Cornwall," Mum giggled. "Back to St Ives, to see all our old friends, Ivy."

"Yay!" Ivy (who'd been named after St Ives) yelped again.

The rest of us didn't yelp. St Ives is a beautiful place, but for me, Linn, Rowan and Tor, it stirred up a weird mix of happy/sad memories. . .

"Can we afford to go on holiday?" I asked, chickening out of bringing up the happy/sad weirdness stuff.

"Not really!" Dad smiled. "But we deserve a family holiday before Linn heads off, because we're all going to miss her badly when she goes to Scotland. . ."

Linn's features softened as an emotional tug pulled at her hidden-away heartstrings.

"*If* I get the grades," she said, with a shrug of her shoulders.

"*You'll* get the grades, Linn!" Mum beamed across the table, first at Linn and then at me. "And, anyway, Ally, it won't be an expensive holiday – we're going to be camping."

Camping?

Linn?

Linn, *camping*?

Ha, ha, ha, ha, ha, ha, ha, ha, ha.

Linn going camping; that would be as weird as sausage-flavoured chocolate. If someone told me that Colin our three-legged cat was planning a parachute jump for charity, it would sound less ridiculous than the idea of my big sister sleeping in a *tent*, of all things.

Without moving my head, I subtly focused the camera in my eye on Linn.

That big fake grin didn't fool me; I knew she was silently wondering if now was a good time to run away from home. . .

Chapter 2

IF YOU'RE NOT HAPPY AND YOU KNOW IT. . .

Probably much to her regret, Linn didn't run away from home.

She spent the next few weeks either working at her summer job (in a posh clothes shop on the Broadway), hanging out with her mates (Alfie, Mary and Nadia) or moping in her room playing her favourite miserable CDs (Coldplay and James Blunt, *endlessly*).

Maybe she'd hoped something would happen before the holiday rolled round; maybe she thought Mum and Dad would have a change of heart and cancel it, or that Cornwall might announce it was unexpectedly closing for repairs or something. But there was no getting out of it . . . today was the day we were setting off. And Linn, wearing a pair of ultra-black shades to hide the bitter resignation in her eyes, was frantically texting her sympathetic girlfriends, who were probably going to hold a candlelit vigil for her over the next week.

Speaking of friends, where were mine? Kyra had

said she'd wander by to say bye-bye, and Billy was supposed to have been here ages ago. I knew he was a dork and had a brain the size of a small peanut which couldn't retain too much information at one time, but he *was* supposed to be my boyfriend, after all.

Still, I wasn't the only boyfriendless Love sister loitering on the pavement outside our house. Rowan (also in dark shades – only hers were purple and heart-shaped) looked lost and glum without Alfie to giggle over. She was perched on her yellow suitcase, as droopy as the trailing pinky-purple fuchsias she'd painted on the sides of it.

I was just about to ask her where Alfie had got to when Grandma sidled up to me.

"Ally, dear," she whispered urgently, "can you help me with something?"

She was holding up a notepad with *Do NUT scratch Flapjack under chin coz he will bit* scribbled on it in my little brother's handwriting.

"What's a flapjack? Apart from a type of cake, of course," she asked, staring worriedly at the instruction (one of many – this was No. 52).

"Flapjack's a name," I explained, as I suddenly spotted Kyra and Billy walking towards the house and gave them a wave. "It's the speckly brown rat."

"Ah. . . Stanley thought a flapjack might be a

variety of chipmunk or something. Still, I have no intention of scratching Tor's rat under the chin or anywhere else. It'll be fed and watered, same as the other pets, while you're away."

Tor was too busy chasing a couple of cats that weren't Colin for a farewell hug to hear Grandma's traitorous words. From Mad Max the hamster to Britney the pigeon, from Kevin the iguana to Cilla the rabbit, from Brian the stick insect to ... er, all the other small, scurrying, fluttering and swimmy things that only Tor could remember the names of, they *all* got a daily snuggle from my little brother (a very careful snuggle in Brian's case). If Tor knew our house was going to be a snuggle-free zone while we were away, chances were he'd dig his small heels in and refuse to go.

"Right, he's said goodbye to everything twice already," Grandma mumbled, gazing at Tor through her gold-rimmed specs. "Think I'll scoop him up and get him belted in before he starts on round three..."

I'd have given her a hand scooping Ivy up too – she kept running back and forth from the house, dragging out more and more toys to take with her – but Kyra and Billy were here now to say their fond farewells.

"God, Ally, it's *awful*!" Kyra groaned loudly, with a look of complete horror on her face. "What *is* it?"

"It's a minibus," I said.

Kyra scrunched up her face in plain disbelief.

"A minibus? But I didn't know they built minibuses back in Roman times!"

Virtually every word that dropped out of Kyra Davies' mouth was coated in sarcasm, so it wasn't a big surprise that she was taking the mick out of the ancient, rusty old banger that Dad had borrowed from his mate Neil to get us – hopefully – all the way to Cornwall. (Kyra had become my best friend by default, since Sandie – my actual best friend – had let me down and moved away to Bath with her family last year.)

"Aren't you going to *die* of embarrassment, being seen in this thing?" Kyra grimaced.

"Well, a stretch limo *might* have been more fun," I shrugged, not keen on admitting that yes, driving along in a a faded mustard-yellow minibus with the lettering "The Sunshine Gospel Steel Band" painted on the side was going to be mortifying. The two reasons I didn't want to admit it were standing about a metre away; Mum and Dad had come out with the last of the bags and were stuffing them in the bus, along with a giggling Ivy, and three excitable dogs.

But I didn't want to fill these last, precious moments with petty worries about people at service stations asking us to play a verse or two of "When The Saints Go Marching In". I hadn't had a chance to say a thing yet to the boy I loved.

"Where've you been, Billy?" I demanded. "You promised to be here half an hour ago!"

"Got you these," said Billy, pulling a bunch of bright pink carnations from behind his back, and blushing hard.

It was a really sweet, really romantic thing to do . . . except for the fact that a) the flowers still had a "reduced to £1.49" sticker on them, b) flowers weren't really a *great* gift to take with you on a six-hour journey, and c) Billy had spoken in a really dumb cartoon voice.

"Thanks," I smiled, chuffed really, despite the cut-price sticker and the uselessness of Billy's present.

"Right, everyone! Let's get going!!" Dad shouted cheerfully.

Linn mustered a semi-convincing smile-ette, let out a sigh and stomped towards her doom – sorry, the minibus – followed by Rowan, her headful of twisty plaits hiding her down-turned face.

"OK, I've got to go," I said hurriedly. "So you know the deal, right? You're not going to forget to text me, are you?"

Of *course* Billy knew the deal. It was his idea for me to beg Linn for two minutes texting-time a day on her mobile, since she was the only one in our family to have one. (She paid for it herself; my right-on, slightly-skint parents think mobiles are about as necessary as hand-knitted space-suits.)

"Don't worry! I won't forget!"

I'd have preferred it if Billy wasn't still doing the cartoon voice (Patrick from *Spongebob Squarepants*, in case you were wondering). I knew what was up; he always does stupid voices or pulls stupid faces when he feels embarrassed.

"Billy! Just give her a kiss, for goodness' sake!" sighed Kyra, also spotting that my boyfriend was hiding his feelings behind a dopey sea slug, or whatever Patrick's meant to be (I've never been able to figure it out).

"Okey-dokey!" Billy answered cheerfully, still in Patrick mode.

I was torn between kissing the big idiot or hitting him over the head with the carnations. I chose the kiss (luckily, he didn't *taste* like a sea slug), and just as well, as all the rest of the Love household was now crammed on board the gospel bus. Stanley was waiting by the back door, gallantly holding it open for me.

"Have a good time!" Kyra called after me, as I grabbed the bag by my feet and hurried off.

"Yeah, have a good time!" croaked Billy/Patrick, sounding like he had a grain of sand or two stuck in his sea slug throat. . .

Blinking madly, I quickly kissed Grandma and Stanley and jumped on board. I grinned and blinked some more as I waved bye to Kyra, who was yawning, and Billy, who was pulling his mouth wide with his fingers and sticking his tongue out at me. Sigh. . . I didn't know whether to laugh, cry or roll my eyes, so I did a little bit of all three.

"Here we go! Everyone excited?" asked Dad, as the minibus chug-chugged off down our street and Dad's favourite punk band (The Clash) burst out of the tinny speakers in the doors.

"Yesssssss!" yelled Ivy, accompanied by some less bouncy "yes"s from the rest of us.

OK, so Linn was *never* going to be excited about this holiday, and Tor and I were temporarily less excited due to ripples of sadness over those we'd left behind (cats, mice, fish, boys disguised as sea slugs), but what was Rowan so glum about? My ditzy sis always saw the world through rose-tinted kaleidescopes, and seeing her deflated and strangely silent was as unnerving and unexpected as seeing Madonna working behind the till in your local petrol station.

But then Rowan was the super-sensitive type, and maybe she was weighed down again with the weirdness of us all going to St Ives – something I'd sort of put on hold at the back of my mind.

Here's the thing: for the four years that Mum was supposedly travelling the world, working out some wanderlust, she'd actually been living in St Ives, having the baby (Dad's) she didn't know she was expecting and a bit of a breakdown into the bargain. The longer Mum had stayed away, she tried to explain later, the harder and harder it got for her to come home. Meanwhile, back in north London, we'd all desperately jumped on the letters and photos she sent, unaware that she'd posed for every snap in deepest Cornwall and got tourists who came into the shop where she worked to post them to us from whichever far-flung exotic location was home to them.

America, Germany, Tahiti, Canada, Portugal, Australia, Iceland. . . It had looked to us like Mum was doing some mad, crazy, *amazing* zigzagging of the world, when all the time, she'd been just a long, meandering train-trip away. How weird was that?

What made Mum turn up in the end was

Grandma's wedding to Stanley (Grandma had known all along where Mum was, and spent *years* trying to get her to get in touch). But Mum was no sooner back than she was gone; not sure how she and Ivy could fit into the family any more.

And that's when we visited St Ives for the first and only time; when Dad and the rest of us launched "Mission: Mum", getting the first train down to St Ives, tracking her down, and practically pinning her to the ground with love and kisses till she realized *that* was all that mattered to any of us.

Mum and Ivy (and of course Ben the Golden Retriever) settled into Crouch End life around about a year ago, and it was hard now to remember any of . . . well, the weirdness. Wasn't visiting there going to let some of the weirdness creep back in? It *had* to be what was making Rowan fold herself up into a stiff, pointy, paper airplane version of herself, hadn't it?

"Is everyone OK with the music?" asked Mum, turning around quickly and making her long goldy hair bounce around her face. "Or shall we have a singalong? What about 'If You're Happy And You Know It?'"

I think Mum was hoping for a simple "yes" or "no", or perhaps another song suggestion. I don't think she – or any of the rest of us – was expecting Rowan to burst into tears.

"Ro! What's *wrong*?!" Mum gasped.

"N – n – n – nothing!" hiccupped Rowan, swiping her tears away, and at the same time swiping swathes of dark eyeshadow and non-waterproof mascara across the bridge of her nose and over her cheeks.

Hmm. If right now was nothing, I'd hate to see Rowan when something was *really* bothering her.

But this whole lot of nothing instantly upset Ivy, who started sniffling in sympathy.

"Oh, Ivy!" exclaimed Mum, unsure which of her daughters to comfort first.

"Oh, *Rolf*!" Tor gasped, as a low pfffffffffffffffttt! sound erupted and a terrible smell filled the minibus.

The ratty minibus, the dread of camping, the duet of sobbing, the odour of dog farts . . . it was enough to drive a girl to banging her head against the window in sheer desperation.

And that's exactly what Linn was doing right now. . .

Chapter 3

A WONDROUSLY RUBBISH IDEA

Imagine saying to your careers teacher, "I really, *really* want to be in the *Tweenies*."

Or, "There's an anti-smoking ad on TV where a man gets to dress up as an evil cigarette – maybe *I* could do something like that?"

Or, "I'd love to do voiceover work; maybe grunt like a Neolithic man on a tourist audiotape for Stonehenge!"

When people go to acting school, and study (verily) worthy stuff like Shakespeare, I bet they don't seriously expect they'll end up squeaking around in a kiddy-show outfit, or sweating inside a giant cigarette, or mumbling prehistorically into a microphone.

But then *someone's* got to do it. I was listening – through headphones – to someone doing it right now. The main, serious-sounding voice I could hear as we wandered around the ancient stone circle of Stonehenge was telling lots of "fascinating" rock-related facts, but in the background, various actors were grunting and clanging pretend tools for atmosphere (they hoped).

Oh, in case you don't know it, Stonehenge is about halfway between London and Cornwall, and Mum and Dad thought it would be a good place to have a break, give praise (hallelujah!) that the gospel bus hadn't broken down yet, and give us Love children a bit of a history lesson at the same time.

Mum, Dad and Tor were strolling ahead of me right now, engrossed in the commentary coming through their headsets. Ivy was more engrossed in skipping along the path, holding Mr Penguin high in the air, making him flap his short, cloth wings and fly. She seemed oblivious to the fact that a) she was a few metres away from one of the most famous landmarks in Britain, and b) penguins don't fly.

Linn was a few footsteps behind, fiddling with her hair; the headphones and the wind swooping across Salisbury Plain were playing havoc with it. Wispy, untidy tendrils were escaping from her super-tight ponytail by the second. (She'd probably take that to be a terrible omen for the holiday.)

As for me, I just wanted to giggle. All the other tourists were shuffling along, staring sombrely at the stones, but instead of thinking, "Wow, I can't believe I'm looking at something built 5,000 years ago!", all that ping!-ed into my mind was, "Wow, did the actors feel like complete dorks when they were in the studio, grunting and groaning and banging on old pots and pans?"

I turned round to look at Rowan and see if she was getting the giggles too, and then realized, no, of course she wasn't. We'd left ditzy Rowan at home, and taken this gloomy version of her on holiday instead. Well, now that I had her to myself, it was the perfect time to quiz her.

"Hey!" I said, tugging at the sleeve of her floaty purple shirt.

"Huh?" she replied.

It wasn't as if she couldn't hear me; she hadn't even bothered to put her headphones on. They were draped around her neck, the wires dangling down her front and getting tangled with the three long strands of beads she'd thrown on this morning.

"What's wrong? I mean *really*?" I asked, slipping my own headphones off and carrying them in one hand.

The reason I'd added that "really" was because I *really* didn't believe the excuse she'd come up with in the minibus earlier for her sudden sob-a-thon.

Not the unconvincing "N – n – n – nothing" excuse, but the one she'd muttered once Mum had *insisted* Ro tell her, or she'd make Dad turn around and go back home (you should have *seen* Linn's eyes light up at that!). So what did Rowan say? Well, she mumbled something about having PMT, which quickly shut Mum up and got her suddenly suggesting a game of "I Spy" to Tor and Ivy. Obviously, it's not as if Mum (being of the female persuasion herself) wasn't sympathetic, but I guess she didn't want to get into explaining periods, and the grumblies you get *before* periods, to an eight-year-old boy and a four-year-old pink person. Actually, I think that's exactly *why* Rowan came up with that particular excuse; she got left alone to stare in a dramatically sad way out of the window.

"*If* I tell you," Rowan said now, in a wide-eyed whisper, "you must promise to tell *no one!*"

Omigod. My sister had become a spy, and knew that she herself – as well as the top-secret government documents hidden in her fuchsia-covered yellow suitcase – were in grave, grave danger from deadly enemy agents. . .

OK, I know none of that was the tiniest bit true. Despite the drama of Rowan's words, she was probably about to admit to going against Mum and Dad's plea for sensible packing and had filled her suitcase full of glitter glue, ribbon and fairy lights.

"Fine. Yes, of course I won't tell," I assured her. "What's up?"

Uh-oh. Even with her purple heart sunglasses on, I could see tears welling up in Rowan's already make-up smudged eyes.

"Ivechuggedaflea," Ro mumbled speedily.

"Huh?" I frowned at her.

Ro looked unhappily uncomfortable, as if I was asking her to shout the colour of the knickers she was wearing to the whole of the ambling Stonehenge crowds.

"I said, I – I've chucked Alfie."

A bewildered goldfish; that's what I must have looked like as I stared at her, my mouth slowly opening and shutting with nothing coming out of it.

"I split up with him last night!!" Ro added, in case I was hard of understanding.

"Huh?" I finally managed to say again (I've got a fantastic vocabulary, as you can plainly see). It wasn't that I hadn't heard her this time, it was just that I couldn't *believe* what I'd just heard.

She'd just chucked *Alfie*? *The* Alfie? The Alfie who was the most . . . well, just *mmmmmmmm* boy on the planet? The boy who I'd had a useless crush on for as long as Linn had been friends with him?

Of course, it was just a pointless crush, since a) I was very happy being Billy's girlfriend, and b) Alfie was four years older than me, so he was more likely to notice a nice pot plant in the house than a sister of Linn's as young as me. . .

But back to Rowan's bombshell.

I'd have to check her immediately for signs of insanity or perhaps even brain death. I mean, how could she randomly go chucking a boy who was gorgeous and nice and (curses for me) mad about her?

Rowan better have a very, very good reason. Maybe Alfie had defaced her precious Johnny Depp posters in a fit of jealousy. Maybe she'd caught him doodling "Alfie ♡ Ally" on a Post-It note (I *wish*).

"You know how he's going to study Humanities at Brighton University after the summer?" she said hurriedly.

"Yes."

Er, *yes* I knew he was going to study Humanities at Brighton University. Except I didn't exactly know what Humanities was (were?). At all.

"Well, I had this brilliant idea, right. . ."

As soon as my airhead sister said she had a brilliant idea, I suspected it was probably a pretty *terrible* idea, whatever it was. When Rowan has a brilliant idea, it's usually about stuff like how to make a stylish hat out of a toilet roll holder, silver foil and sequins.

". . .of going with him!!" she finished, her face brightening a little as she looked at me expectantly. Expecting me to say, "What an inspired amazing idea!", I think. But all I said instead was. . .

"Huh?" (See what I mean about my stunning vocabulary?)

"Well, there's supposed to be this market place somewhere in an area called North Lanes or something, and you can hire a stall, and sell your arty crafty things. Yeah?"

Mmm. So far, so vague.

"Uh, yeah," I mumbled, checking to see if the warm wind blowing across Salisbury Plain was actually blowing straight through both Rowan's ears without encountering any obstacles, such as brain matter.

"So I said to Alfie, what if I just get a stall, and make stuff for it, and then I could live in Brighton with you?!"

Urgh. This wasn't sounding good at *all*. Let me get this straight: Rowan wanted to leave home, leave us, give up her plans to go to study fashion at art school, and live in Brighton, renting a stall in a market "somewhere" in an area called North Lanes "or something", where she'd sell "stuff" she'd made.

"What sort of stuff?" I asked tentatively.

"*I* don't know!" said Rowan, as if I'd just asked the dumbest of questions. "That's not the *point*, Ally. . . The point is, Alfie told me, well, it was a *stupid* idea!! Can you *believe* that? So what could I do? I *had* to chuck him!"

Oh, dear. My sister was battier than a cricket bat, a ping-pong bat and a fruit bat put together. She was the princess of rubbish ideas, but this was a wondrously rubbish idea, even for her.

"Hunughhh," I mumbled, hoping that mumble would sound enough like an answer to satisfy her while every cell in my body was shouting, "She's *mad*!!"

"But *no one* knows, Ally. Before Alfie left, I asked him not to speak to Linn about it till *I* did. And I'm not doing that till we get home from holiday – I couldn't stand it."

I sort of saw Rowan's point: Linn had – kind of understandably – never been keen on Alfie and Rowan going out. It would be bad enough (for Ro) if Linn found out back at home, where there was the whole house, the whole of Crouch End, and actually the whole of London to get away from each other in. But on holiday, in the space of a tent . . . oh.

That's oh as in "oh, dear" and "oh, no". In capitals and with lots of exclamation marks. Suddenly, I was so glad that I was me and Billy was a sea slug, and our relationship was so nice and easy and funny.

"Promise you'll keep it a secret, Ally? Promise? Don't tell Mum or Dad either, 'cause they'll try to be nice and talk to me, and then Linn'll get to hear, and . . . and. . ."

Rowan ran out of words and blinked pleadingly at me from behind her purple hearts.

"I promise," I told her, giving her hand a squeeze to show I meant it. (Rowan might be as mad as a deranged fish, but she was also sad and miserable and my sister, after all.)

At the same time, I made another promise to myself: while Linn and Rowan, for their own reasons, weren't going to have a good time on this holiday, I definitely *was*, along with my bouncy, lovely, irrepressible little brother and sister. Oh, and the dogs.

Yep, for the next week, I was determined to be as goofily happy as Rolf, Winslet and Ben. Only without the bum-sniffing, farting and doggy-chunks breath, of course. . .

Chapter 4

THE FAMOUS LEANING TENTS OF ST IVES

"Monsters are coming!! Run *awayyyyyyy*!!" shouted Tor.

"*Aaaaiiieeeeeeeeeeeee!!*" shrieked Ivy.

A blur of little boy and pink girl zoomed between the tents, followed by three happily lolloping dogs, who had no idea they were supposed to be monsters.

Now about those tents. . . There were three of them, each facing in, like the points of a squint triangle. Thanks to general ancientness and random missing guy ropes and pegs, they all looked slightly drunk. The biggest of the drunk tents was for Mum, Dad, Tor and Ivy. The two-man tent (which Rowan was currently customizing with large felt flowers, dangling homemade mobiles and a fairy mascot) was going to be home-sweet-home to me and Ro for the next week. The smallest of the three was just for one; a perfect grouch-pod for Linn.

"Whoops!" laughed Mum's pal Val, trying to get

out of the way of the monster game and nearly tripping over a coolbox.

Val had wasted no time coming here to see Mum and us, though she may have wished she'd left it for half an hour so that she didn't get roped into helping put the tents up. Her brother Daniel (more on him in a sec) had helped out too, and was now standing around with Dad, as Mum and Val did speed-chatting and catching up.

Now that the tents were up, I'd thought about unpacking my bag and unfurling my sleeping bag, but I reckoned I might get in Rowan's way and end up with a felt flower stuck to my forehead with fabric glue.

Instead I sat down, safely out of the monster-and-victims-and-felt-flowers' way and started scribbling. So far I'd written eight Stonehenge-pictured postcards: one for Grandma and Stanley (of course), one for Colin the three-legged cat at home (because I'm mad), one for Kyra (Miss Sarcasm), one for Sandie (my long-lost best friend), and one each for Chloe, Salma, Jen and Kellie (my second division mates back in Crouch End).

Now, of course, it was Billy's turn.

Hey you –
We are camping quite near the middle of nowhere.

*Tents are wobbly. Linn on verge of strop. Having a
lovely time (ha!).*
From ME!! xxxx
PS Know it's corny, but wish you were here.

I'd last seen Billy my boyfriend exactly seven
hours and ten minutes ago. I tried to picture what
he might be doing: as it was late Saturday
afternoon, I supposed he might be at Ally Pally
skatepark with his mates right now, or maybe he'd
be at home, taking his mind off missing me by
blowing things up on one of his Xbox games.

And here I was, far, far away, leaning on a rock to
write my message, as there were no picnic tables
around. There wasn't *anything* much around on
this campsite, mainly because we weren't *on* a
campsite, we were in a field. With grass. And the
distant waft of cowpats lingering in the air.

Oh, yes, we weren't only going to save money on
this holiday by camping, we were going to save
even *more* by camping on the cheap, on a bit of
spare farmland that belonged to Val's brother
Daniel. Maybe it would've been useful for us Love
children to know this piece of information in
advance (so we could maybe panic a bit), but then
Mum said she thought *Dad* had told us, and Dad
said he thought *Mum* had told us.

Y'know, I did have this sneaking suspicion that they'd talked about it earlier and made a pact not to say anything, simply because they knew some of us *would* panic. . .

"Where's the bathroom?"

Uh-oh. The Grouch Queen had most definitely hit the panic button. Linn was standing eerily still, her dainty floral toilet bag swinging forlornly from one hand. There was a look of confused disbelief in her eyes, like a driver who comes out of a shop and finds their car's been towed away.

I might sound like I was taking the mickey out of Linn, but it was actually a valid question. A quick glance around showed grass, more grass, a rickety barn, a small copse of trees, a country lane that (eventually) meandered its way to St Ives, and more grass.

"Ha!" Daniel laughed.

He seemed like a nice bloke; tall, skinny and smiley, a male version of his sister Val. And Daniel *must've* been nice, because a) he'd let us stay here for free, b) he'd helped put up the tents, and most importantly c) he was a (past-life) friend of Mum's. But with that one, careless "ha!" in Linn's direction, I knew instantly that Daniel had suddenly become a new entry on her mental list of irritating people and things.

"There's no bathroom *here*!" He laughed some more, making him instantly shoot up to number one on Linn's Irritation List. "There's just an outdoor toilet at the side of the barn there. And a standpipe too, for water, of course!"

Of course.

I was glad for Daniel's sake that Linn wasn't armed with any dangerous weapons. Though she *was* clutching those straighteners in quite a threatening manner. . .

"*Where*," she said, struggling to keep her voice even, "am I meant to plug *these* in?"

Please don't laugh again, I silently urged Daniel.

He laughed. Linn's nostrils flared.

"Oh, *you* can do without straighteners for a week, Linn, darling!" Mum smiled nervously.

I shot a quick look at Rowan, who'd instantly thought the same thing as me: expecting Linn to do without straighteners was sheer madness. It was like asking someone who couldn't walk if they'd mind swapping their wheelchair for a cardboard box for a week.

"Um, what about showers?" I asked, wandering over to join the discussion (and ready to disarm Linn if necessary – she might try and throttle someone with the cable).

"Oh, I'm sure we'll manage with just basins of

water from the standpipe," said Mum. "We can heat up water in pans on the campfire."

"Yeah," Dad nodded. "It'll be a laugh – a real adventure!"

A laugh? It'd be more like one of those reality shows where they make people live like nineteenth-century settlers in America. Dad would be suggesting we whittle our own toothbrushes next.

"Well, if any of you get fed up of the standpipe, feel free to come up to the house for a shower if you like." Daniel pointed to a pin-prick of a farmhouse further up the lane. "You could come plug your hair thing in there too, Linnhe. You can use my daughter's room – she won't mind."

Linn bristled. What a dilemma: an offer she couldn't refuse from the person who'd so deservingly entered her Irritation List at number one. And to add insult to injury, he'd used her proper name. She hated the fact that she'd been called after a Scottish loch. I think it was something to do with the fact that lochs, lakes and ponds filled her mind with yucky images of silt, algae, fish spawn and assorted muddy gloop.

"Oh. . .! Where've Tor and Ivy got to?" Mum suddenly asked, alerted to their disappearance by the eerie lack of squealing and accompanying woofs.

Linn instantly forgot her straightener woes and glanced around sharply, same as the rest of us.

"Tor? Ivy?" Mum called out.

We all froze and listened, hearing only the drone of a distant tractor.

"TOR! IVY! WHERE ARE YOU?!" Dad now bellowed, while I ran to check the tents, and Rowan did the same with the gospel van.

But like the tents, the van was empty except for the odd fly buzzing around.

"I'll look in the barn," I heard Daniel say, as I backed out of the one-man, no-kids tent.

"Where could they have gone?" Mum asked in an edge-of-shrill voice, her long, cotton skirt spinning out around her ankles as she swivelled round and round and surveyed the empty field.

It was totally unlikely that in the few minutes we'd been talking toilets, someone would have managed to kidnap two small children and three lolloping dogs (mainly because no cars had passed in the lane, and the dogs would have turned from soppy hounds to demented guard dogs if anyone had tried to lay a finger on my brother and sister). But still, you couldn't help thinking that way, could you? It was like the time last year when me and my sisters took Tor to the crowded market at Camden Lock and managed to lose him. Course, while our stomachs were full of knots and our brains were a tangle of worry, he'd been in a world of his own, rescuing an injured pigeon, completely unaware that me, Ro and Linn were first going to kill him and then hug him to death when we were finally reunited.

Ah . . . Britney. (That's our pet pigeon; Tor nursed her back to health and released her in the garden, which she's never left since.) Thinking of Britney made me wonder if this current disappearance was in any way animal-related. I was about to suggest that when Val blurted out in alarm: "God, I just remembered! There's a stream in that copse over there!"

A second later, anyone watching from a distant tractor/glider/spaceship might have thought, *How charming! All those people are having a lovely race!* And I guess it *was* a kind of race; a race against time in case the kids and the dogs had all somehow managed to fall in the river during their frantic chasing game. The dogs might be able to doggy paddle their way to safety, but Tor and Ivy were still too wary to ditch their armbands at the local pool.

With horrible, water-related what-ifs swimming through all our minds, everyone sprinted as fast as they could. The trainer-wearers (me and Dad) got to the trees a few seconds ahead of the Birkenstock (Val) and sandal-wearers (Mum, Ro, Linn).

We stood wheezing painful breaths, gazing down at something that luckily wasn't so much a stream as a babbling, ankle-deep brook. And instead of drowning kids and dogs, there was a small boy talking to a frog, three snuffling, soaking, water-lapping pooches, and a brown Ivy.

That's right; a brown Ivy, singing her mud song.

"Hey!" she grinned, suddenly spotting us all. "Guess what I am? I'm a hippopot—"

Before she could say "—amus", Linn had hurtled from behind us, selflessly slithered down the bank, and pulled Ivy to safety in her arms. It was only once the ankle-deep mud started oozing into her sandals and the brown Ivy started wriggling and giggling that it dawned on Linn that Ivy hadn't needed rescuing after all; she'd been enjoying her hippo mudbath game.

"Awww! You all scared it away!" said Tor indignantly, as the frog boinged off the rock it had been perched on and sploshed into the water. "He was my new friend!"

"*I'll* find him!" said brown Ivy, slithering out of Linn's arms, leaving a trailed imprint of herself all over Linn's white vest top and khaki short skirt.

A huge, rumbling giggle suddenly made my

chest begin to heave. I had to use practically super-human powers to hold it in, even if the rest of my family and Val were now laughing at the spectacle of Linn, out of pure relief.

My struggle paid off. Linn glowered daggers at everyone else, but blinked a thank you at me for my solidarity, especially when I held my hand out to help her up.

What a nice sister I was. A good Samaritan, even.

Well, OK, a good actress, then.

Boy, I didn't want to risk the wrath of Linn and risk losing those precious, daily two-minutes worth of texting she'd promised me. . .

Chapter 5

THE DREADED SHACK-OF-A-HUT-OF-A-LOO

Ivy was in love. With a pair of wellies.

It hadn't been love at first sight; Ivy had been determined to have an all-pink pair (*quelle surprise*, as Mr Matthews my French teacher would say – usually in a sarky tone when someone told him they'd forgotten to bring their homework). But small girls can't be choosers, specially when it's August and the shops are full of flip-flops and sunglasses.

Ivy had finally settled on a leaf-green pair with a pink – phew – trim, which she wore all the way from our quick shopping trip to St Ives to the luxurious splendour of our holiday location (i.e. the field).

"Do you want to take them off now?" Mum asked Ivy, as we sat around the campfire on cushions, eating fruit salad with white Chocolate Buttons. (That was one of Rowan's foodie ideas that went spectacularly right – she more normally made us gag with inventive disasters like peanut butter and mayonnaise sandwiches or mince and carrot soup.)

"Nope," said our little sis, shaking her brown bob emphatically. "They look nice with my pyjamas."

Mum hadn't got Ivy the wellies as replacement slippers; they were what Ivy had promised to wear if she went playing in the muddy brook from now on. (Ivy and Tor had also promised not to go there again without someone considerably bigger tagging along and keeping an eye on them.) Anyway, late this afternoon, we'd left Dad to potter at the campsite/field with Tor, while us Love girlies had wandered into St Ives on the welly hunt, being pointed to likely shops by Val, who was on her way back to her craft shop to see how busy or not business had been.

"Aren't you two feeling tired yet?"

Dad's question was aimed at Tor and Ivy of course; we knew that without him having to turn round from the radio he was fiddling with. Something that sounded jangly and poppy and African suddenly jumped out of the tiny speakers, nicely drowning out the low, idling rumble of the gospel bus's engine.

"Nope," said Tor and Ivy in unison, looking ridiculously perky, and in serious danger of staying up *way* too late due to over-excitement and an overload of Chocolate Buttons.

Also, you couldn't blame them for wanting to stay up. Between them, my parents (and Rowan, of course) had made our little camp gorgeous. Mum had hung up homemade, multi-coloured paper chains, linking and criss-crossing them between all three tents. From a box of supplies brought from the kitchen at home, she'd rustled up a special seaside-themed Saturday night tea – quiche decorated with spinach "seaweed" and carrot "clownfish". Before she'd called us all over for tea (me, my sisters and Tor had been watching Ivy test-drive her wellies in the brook), Mum had laid out hand-scribbled nameplates on each cushion on the grass, and then given us crêpe paper starfish garlands to wear while we ate.

And now that the sky was a beautiful, meandering muddle of blues, mauves and sunsetting peach, Dad had got in on the act and put tea lights in the painted jam jars Mum had brought along, as well as rigging up the minibus's battery to somehow power the fairy lights Rowan had insisted on taking. (Where had she planned to plug them in? A bush?)

"Anything back from Billy yet?" I found myself turning and checking with Linn, who was sitting –

bolt upright – on the neighbouring cushion to me.

She looked irked. No surprise, I suppose, since it was about the seventy-fifth time I'd asked her. In the last hour, I mean.

"No."

"Could you maybe just check?" I asked hopefully.

"Ally, my mobile is in my pocket. If it bleeps a message, I'll be able to hear it."

"Uh, yeah, but you know what it's like. . . If your phone is in your pocket, you might just move and accidentally flip the button to mute or vibrate or something, and you won't realize you've got a message!"

I knew I was annoying her, but I couldn't stop myself. It had been fifty-three minutes since I'd taken advantage of my two-minute text time and written "*Going 2 the beach 2morrow – hope I see a sea slug, coz it'll remind me of u*", and I was dying to see what silliness Billy was going to reply with. We weren't very good at romantic, whispering-sweet-nothings, pass-the-sick-bucket stuff; we showed how much we cared by being as cheeky as we could to each other, most of the time.

"My mobile *isn't* going to change settings, Ally." Linn sighed. "If I get a message, I'll let you know. OK?"

"OK," I muttered, feeling a huge squeeze of something in my stomach; a big missing-Billy moment, I guess. I took a peek at Rowan to see if she was missing a certain someone too. . . I supposed the answer might be yes, since she seemed to be swooshing her spoon round and round in her bowl without actually eating anything (a crime in my eyes, when you're talking fruit and white Chocolate Buttons).

"Oh . . . what about this?" asked Dad, tuning the radio in again to something that *might* have sounded really nice except for the squeal of static that suddenly shot through the warm evening air, instantly disturbing three dozing dogs and making them bark and whine.

"Shsshh! You'll wake the neighbours!" Mum giggled, pointing to the faraway, twinkly lights in the farmhouse windows.

"Or wake the children," said Linn, nodding over at two suddenly snoozling bundles on the cushions.

"How do little kids do that?" I asked, as Mum leant over to grab a sideways-slithering bowl from Ivy's lap.

"I know; how can they sometimes be so awake one minute and totally asleep the next?" asked Dad, scooping up Tor, while I beat Mum and my sisters to it and began lifting Ivy. "You were exactly the same, Ally Pally – once, when you must've been round about three, you fell asleep in the middle of a wee. I turned around to get a new roll of loo paper out of the cupboard, and when I turned back you had your head on your knees and were snoring!"

As I bent down and gently manoeuvred myself and Ivy into the opening of the dark main tent, I gave a ton of silent thanks that Dad had never told that story in front of Billy or Kyra. It would give them ammunition for *years*. . .

"Have you checked this out, by the way?" said Dad, following me into the tent with Tor, and somehow flipping on a torch with a spare finger. At first, I thought he meant the joint cuteness of the two junior ready-beds; one with Clifford the Big Red Dog on it (Ivy's) and one with saucer-eyed seal cubs (Tor's). But then I realized that Dad was pointing to three rows of photos taped to the canvas wall. Carefully sliding Ivy into her bed, I leant over and took a closer look; it was a bunch of mostly blurry, finger-interrupting snaps of all the pets back at home.

"He said it would help him not to miss them so much." Dad grinned at me.

Aw, Tor. . . I couldn't do much about Linn's

moping or Rowan's secret sadness, but one thing was for sure, I could help the little guys have the best fun ever during this holiday, and that included watching for signs of pet-yearning on Tor's part. If that happened, maybe I could arrange for Grandma to put the phone next to a cage or two, so that Tor could hear the reassuring sound of hamster wheels squeaking and stick insects . . . er . . . crunching on leaves or something.

"Maybe it'd be better if we took *these* off." Dad laughed, tapping on a rubbery lump or two at the foot of the Clifford bed cover.

I left him separating green-and-pink wellies from a dead-to-the-world Ivy as I backed out of the tent and turned to see Mum . . . and no one else but a lazing dog or three.

"Linn and Rowan are both off to their tents; they said they felt tired." Mum shrugged at me.

I knew she was wondering if I knew what was wrong with them, but she wasn't about to ask, since tents are not exactly known for their sound-proofing, and the gentle country-ish channel Mum had now tuned the radio into wasn't going to be loud enough to drown out any private conversation.

"Oh," I said, feeling strangely pleased at the news that my sisters had "retired" for the night. But then it wasn't so strange; the idea of sitting around with Linn and Ro and their individual auras of gloom didn't sound like a whole heap of Saturday night fun. What *might* be Saturday night fun was to have Mum and Dad all to myself, for once. That's the trouble with big families, isn't it? You only get slivers of time with your parents, disjointed conversations that are interrupted by someone saying they've put a purple skirt in with the whites and accidentally dyed all Linn's tops mauve (Rowan), or asking if you can phone the tooth fairy cause they've got a loose tooth (Tor), or letting you know they've just eaten an ant (Ivy).

I realized it would be really lovely to sit and chat with Mum and Dad, and maybe listen to them tell funny stories about us all. Preferably no more embarrassing ones about me and toilets, though. . .

Speaking about toilets, before I could relax and enjoy this, I'd have to brave the trek to the dreaded outdoor loo before it got any darker. The loo by the barn was yucky enough by daylight (there was no running water; just a bucket you had to refill to "flush", and only a view of the field where a window should be).

"Can I borrow that night light, Mum? I've got to go. . ."

Mum picked up a crimson-painted jam jar with

string wrapped round the rim and passed it over.

"Want company?" she asked.

"Nah." I shook my head.

Of *course* I wanted her to come, but I also suddenly wanted to feel like an adult who was going to sit down with two other adults for a good chat in a few minutes' time.

"Well, borrow Rolf, then," she smiled, gently shoving the long-legged scruffbucket to his sleepy feet.

"Thanks," I said, setting off across the grass with my pool of pinky light, a faithful dog by my side and a knot of dread in my stomach.

Three minutes later and I was there, in the shack-of-a-hut-of-a-loo, sitting on the edge of the nasty plastic seat, willing my now-reluctant bladder to hurry up and get on with it. Rolf was in no hurry; no sooner had I pulled the wooden door closed with the rope handle (mmm, classy!), than he'd flopped on the floor and continued with his napping.

"Why isn't there a lock on this thing?" I muttered to keep myself company.

"'Cause it's in the middle of a field in the middle of nowhere," I answered myself. "There's hardly going to be a queue, is there?"

I looked out of the open window on my left,

and saw a whole heap of darkness. Only a letterbox-slither of orange on the horizon gave out any colour in the inkiness. I wasn't used to that: in our corner of north London, the street lights twinkle into the distance as far as you can see, and you can see an awful lot of twinkling lights if you go up to Alexandra Palace, the big, rambling old building on the hill close to my house. You should be up there on Fireworks Night; wow. Not only do they put on a huge, dazzling, chest-booming show in the grounds, but you can see firework displays erupting like shooting stars all over the city.

A memory suddenly wormed its way into my head. It was a Fireworks Night a few years ago; one of the ones we went to when Mum wasn't around. Me and Tor and Dad were up for having a great time, racing to write our names in the air with sparklers before the main show started. Then another unexpected show started up and put a dampener on things; the Linn and Rowan show. Linn went mental, 'cause Rowan was waving a homemade glittery wand around in time to the Oasis track that was booming out of the tannoys on the hill. It wasn't the waving that got on Linn's wick, or the fact that Rowan waved it too much and got it tangled in Linn's ponytail.

The problem was more that Rowan had made her wand approximately five seconds before we came out, and the glitter glue she used was still wet. . .

So Linn had shouted, Rowan had cried and stormed off home, and then we *all* had to follow and miss the fireworks when Dad realized only *he* had the keys to the house.

Linn and Rowan, Rowan and Linn. It was funny (well, *not* funny, actually) how much their moods could affect the rest of us.

Like this holiday. . . The way they were going, they'd both end up being little clouds in this sunshine-y place. And that wasn't fair to Mum and Dad, who'd planned it as a treat and couldn't really afford it. And it wasn't fair on the little guys, who just wanted to run around (possibly in wellies) and have fun.

And hey, *I* wanted to have fun too.

Sitting there in the shack-of-a-hut-of-a-loo, with a light breeze drifting through the window and chilling my bum, I reminded myself of the promise I'd made earlier: to have a good time, even if Linn and Rowan didn't plan to. In fact, I decided that whatever happened, I was going to ignore it, rise above it, and not let *anyone*, or *anything* spoil my week!

That profound thought zapped into my head exactly a half a second before Rolf lifted his head and started growling, and a full second before the shack-of-a-hut-of-a-loo door was yanked open and two strange faces stared in at me. . .

Chapter 6

IT WAS ALL JUST A DREAM . . . (NOT)

I felt like a butterfly who'd got into a bit of bother.

All the other butterflies had slowly shaken their wings, and with a soft *pop*! had escaped from their cocoons and gracefully fluttered up to meet the petals of fragrant flowers.

And there *I* was, sticky, stuck and wriggling uselessly in my cocoon, wishing they gave out escape plans and very small butterfly-sized Swiss Army knives with these things. . .

The chatting, giggling and barking outside finally did it; seeping into my sleepy senses till I blinked myself awake and realized I wasn't a trapped butterfly at all (phew). Instead I was a sticky, stuck, uselessly wriggling fourteen-year-old, who was so tangled up in her sleeping bag she looked like a girl-flavoured Twister ice cream.

Never mind, I thought, as I inched my hand out bit-by-sweaty-bit, and aimed for the zip and freedom. If the butterfly thing was just a dream, then perhaps the other thing was too; the stupid thing my subconscious had come up with. Y'know, that dumb scene where total strangers walked into the shack-of-a-hut-of-a-loo and caught me with my pants down.

Or, I suddenly realized with shame beaming into my cheeks (the ones on my *face*, actually), *I didn't dream that bit at all. . .*

With the zip finally forced down a little, I slowly and uncomfortably squiggled myself out of the sleeping bag, trying all the time to sort out the facts from the fuzzy stuff in my still sleepy brain. And bit-by-painful-bit, everything started to become clearer. . .

- Today was Sunday, our first full day on holiday.
- The reason I felt muggy and fuggy was because I'd been kept awake by the stupid, tiny, breeze-jangling bells that Rowan had attached to the outside of our tent.
- And it wasn't just Rowan's bells that had disturbed my sleep; it was Rowan too. She'd tossed and turned all night, sniffling and snuffling and sleep-wittering about Alfie.
- The horrible, seeping realization that the incident in the shack-of-a-hut-of-a-loo was as real as real could be. . .

"And they were definitely both teenagers, right?"

Mum had said last night, as soon as the gawping strangers had hurried off giggling in the dark, and I'd hurtled back to the safety of the camp with trusty Rolf and my tail between my legs.

"Yes." I'd nodded, trying hard not to remember the surprised-but-deeply-amused looks on the faces of the boy and the girl staring in at me.

"They must be locals. I bet they saw the glow of your jam jar and wondered what was going on," Mum had ruminated, passing me comfort food in the shape of leftover Chocolate Buttons, while Dad and the dogs wandered around with a torch, trying to sniff out visitors of the unexpected kind. "I bet you gave those two as much of a scare as they gave you!"

"Yeah, but *they* didn't have their knickers around their knees. . ." I'd mumbled before crawling off to bed to sleep off my shame.

Well, I thought now, crawling back out of the tent into the blinking morning sunlight, *at least I'll probably never see those people again.*

"Till now. . ." I mumbled, staring up at two grinning teenagers standing either side of Daniel as he chatted to my parents.

I guess it was less embarrassing than last night – at least I had more clothes on this time. But then again, I was on all fours, wearing a scuzzy pair of grey tracksuit bottoms and an old T-shirt with a kitten on the front. The kitten T-shirt might have looked kitsch and cute, if I hadn't got bored one night and drawn a pair of glasses and a moustache on it with a marker pen that had never washed off.

"Aha! Ally Pally! Woken up at last, Sleeping Beauty?" Dad smiled a beaming smile at me. "Come and meet some people. . . This is Daniel's son and daughter."

They were tall and slim like their dad, but the blonde highlights in the girl's brown hair came from a posh hairdresser rather than inherited genes. The boy looked like he spent a few quid on products too – his hair was spiked up on top in a mini fin.

"This is Sol," said Daniel, laying a hand on the boy's shoulder, "and this is Lana."

Anyone else might have thought the two teenagers were giving me broad, friendly grins, but *I* knew they were imagining me in a compromising position.

"I heard what happened last night," Daniel continued. "Sorry you got caught out, Ally! It's just that they're only here on holiday for a week with me, and they forgot I mentioned you guys were camping here."

"Sol and Lana were just explaining that they'd been in St Ives, and were cycling home," said Mum, taking over from Daniel. "They both needed to use the loo and couldn't wait till they got to the farmhouse, so they'd left their bikes on the lane and raced each other over to the barn – where they accidentally walked in on you!"

Mum, Dad, Daniel, Sol and Lana . . . they were all looking down at me, waiting for me stand up and/or say something. But in the (mortifying) circumstances, what *could* I say? "Hey, I totally understand! No hard feelings!", or maybe "No worries. Feel free to walk in on me anytime!"

Instead, I started to back into my tent, mumbling something about getting dressed.

And I stayed inside, overheating in my canvas cocoon, till I finally heard Daniel and co. leaving.

If I never saw those two knowing, grinning faces again, it would be too soon. . .

But thanks to my mum, "never" lasted about ten minutes.

I guess she was just trying to be sweet and thoughtful and kind when she invited Sol and Lana to hang out with us down at the beach, while their dad was busy on the farm. It just wasn't very sweet, thoughtful and kind in connection with *me*.

"Oh! You don't *mind*, do you, Ally?" she'd asked

me in a panic, as soon as Sol and Lana went back to the farmhouse to pick up their swimsuits and whatever.

"Hnumphhhh. . ." I'd mumbled and shrugged, since it was a bit late to do anything about it.

Maybe it wouldn't be so bad, I suddenly decided. Maybe I should hope for the best, like getting knocked down by a car on the way to the Porthmeor beach and spending the rest of my holiday in hospital, safely away from the knowing grins I'd probably have to endure off and on for the next six days. . .

Chapter 7

LET'S BE FRIENDS – I DON'T THINK

Being away from St Ives for a year or so had left serious gaps in Mum's memory.

For example, she'd forgotten the names of some of the friendly faces who'd waved and said hi to her on the way to the beach. And speaking of the beach, she hadn't remembered that there was a ban on dogs on all the main St Ives beaches in the summer. What a doggy bummer.

Rolf, Winslet and Ben certainly weren't too thrilled to be watching people digging holes in the sand and splashing in the sea when they couldn't join in. Tor wasn't too thrilled at seeing his dogs tied up to a lamp post either. He was itching to take them back to the field, and I'd offered to go with him, but Mum and Dad had insisted that the dogs would be OK for an hour, and that we should just try to have a good time now we were here.

So I threw myself into making monster sandcastles with Tor and Ivy, and studiously kept my back to Sol and Lana. But then Dad blew my cover by offering to take the kids for ice creams. I nearly went too, till it occurred to me that Billy still owed me a text. Time to check in with Linn and her mobile. . .

"Ouch!" I yelped, as a yellow frisbee cracked me on the shin. (Oh, and *no*, I hadn't managed to get splatted on the road on the way here, although I was tempted when I saw a speeding ice-cream van hurtling down the lane at one point. The only thing that put me off was thinking that the van could kill me, and my family might choose to play "Teddy Bear's Picnic" at my funeral, since it was the last sound I ever heard, tinkling out of the ice-cream van's loudspeaker. How tragic would *that* be?)

"Ha, ha, ha! You're supposed to *catch* the frisbee, you idiot!" laughed Sol, hands on his hips, T-shirt off, and bare, tanned torso on show.

"I'm not *in* your game, so why would I know to catch it?" I frowned his way, chucking the frisbee back across the sands towards him, and hoping I'd aimed for his head. (Missed. Drat.)

But anyway, what did Sol think he was doing? Striking the (not-quite) six-pack pose, I mean? Was he hoping to get spotted by some teen mag; for one of those "Hunks in Trunks"/"Beach Boy Babes" features they always have at this time of year?

When I was helping Mum get the kids into their swimsuits earlier, she'd tried to fill me in on some Sol and Lana info, in an attempt to get me more interested in them, I think. Apparently, Lana was seventeen, Sol was fifteen, they lived with their mum in Yorkshire and didn't have any mates here in town, since their dad had only moved here five years ago and they didn't spend much more than a week here and there with him. I can't say I was surprised about the no-mates thing – the way Lana was languishing on her towel, all aloof and bored and plugged into her MP3 player right now, she didn't look exactly up for getting to know people. And Sol . . . well, Sol just seemed so loud and full of himself that no one else would get a word in edgeways anyhow. Except for maybe *one* person. . .

"Sol! *Sol!!*" Rowan called out to him, jumping up and down barefoot, and waving her arms with a manic tinkle of bracelets. "Over to me!"

Sol caught the spinning frisbee with ease, gave me a cheeky wink (yuck!) and spun it onwards to his new mate Rowan.

"*She* seems to be having a good time," came a mutter from behind a copy of *Memoirs of a Geisha*.

I hadn't realized that Linn had even noticed what was going on; as I'd walked towards her, I could've sworn she was totally engrossed in her new book. She must've been peeking over the top, spy-style.

"Mmm. . ." I muttered, perching myself on the sturdy coolbox beside her.

I had to admit, I was pretty confused by Rowan. I mean, only *I* knew about her break-up with Alfie, but as far as I was concerned, she was meant to be moping over him, not getting matey with someone she'd known for about seven seconds.

"Funny that Ro's been miserable up till now, and then the *minute* a boy starts showing her some attention. . ."

"Yeah, but she's not exactly going to *fancy* him, is she?" I said to Linn, catching on to what she was hinting at. "He's a whole year younger than her for a start!"

"Whatever, she's still acting all giggly and girly with him. . ." Linn said disapprovingly, thinking – I suppose – about her mate Alfie. (Didn't seem like she knew it was over, so Alfie must've kept his promise to Rowan and not told Linn.)

"Maybe she's just trying to be friendly," I suggested, trying to convince myself. "I think Mum's pretty keen on us being friendly to Sol and Lana, since they're Daniel's kids."

Yeah, like me and the two people who'd

sniggered at me in a horribly vulnerable moment could be great friends – I *don't* think. Actually, right now, it was as if all that matey stuff was more important to Mum than me and my mortified feelings. . .

"Hmm, maybe." Linn shrugged. "But that Sol's quite obnoxious, isn't he?"

"Do you think so?" I asked. I mean, yeah, *I* certainly got that impression, but up until that second I didn't know if anyone else in my family did.

"Mmm – he was making these terrible beached whale jokes when we passed that big bloke on the way down here. Didn't you hear him?"

"No." I hadn't heard, and I hadn't seen any big bloke either; I'd spent the whole walk down reliving the toilet trauma of last night and trying to will myself invisible. "What did Mum and Dad say about that?"

"Nothing – they didn't hear. Rowan laughed, though."

We both stared at our sister again. Who knows what Linn was thinking exactly, but *I* suddenly found myself wondering if accidentally sniffing too much glitter glue had destroyed the part of Rowan's brain that dealt with reason and common sense.

"By the way, Ally," Linn said, turning to face me full on, "did you come over here to talk to me, or to use my mobile?"

"Um, both," I fibbed slightly. "Any texts from Billy?"

"Nope."

"Um, can I have my two minutes now, please? And can I *phone* Billy instead of texting him?"

Since Billy hadn't got back to last night's text, I didn't want to send off another one into silent cyberspace: I needed to hear he was there and OK with my own ears.

"Even with a phone call, it's *still* two minutes," Linn warned, looking at me sternly over the top of her sunglasses and holding up the watch she'd taken off to avoid strap marks in her tan.

(Speaking of a tan, her nose was looking on the pinky side of burnt to me. But I didn't dare mention it, in case she got in a huff and reduced my phone time to half a second.)

"Two minutes; of course," I nodded, tapping in Billy's number and waiting impatiently for a reply.

And then there it was, sort of.

"Hi! *Ow* – gerroff!! Now! *Down!!*"

"Billy! It's me!" I grinned, feeling warm and fuzzy inside at hearing the sound of his ordinary, non-cartoon voice and the shrill yapping of his horrible toy poodle dog in the background. "Where are you?"

"In the park."

Ah, the park round Alexandra Palace, where me and Billy met to walk our posse of dogs every Sunday. I suddenly felt a huge twang of home-sickness.

"Precious!" Billy yelped. "I said NO! Get your nose *out* of there!"

"What's Precious doing?"

"Trying to eat my shorts."

"Huh?"

"Well, trying to eat the bit of ham sandwich I've got in my pocket."

That should be an entertaining sight for anyone else strolling through the park, I thought.

"There you go, you stupid mutt. It's on the ground – eat it. Happy now? So . . . how's it going, Ally?" he said more calmly, now that he'd dislodged his dog's snout from his groin area. "Linn still being a total moan-head?"

I immediately pressed the phone closer to my head and hoped my sis hadn't heard that, or else it would be a case of never mind half a second; my daily phone access was likely to be cut to less-than-zero. Luckily, Linn still seemed pretty intent on pretending to read her book while studying Rowan and Sol as they buffooned around athletically with the frisbee.

"Mmm," I mumbled in answer, hoping Billy would pick up the fact that I couldn't talk. He did.

"She's right there, isn't she?"

"Mmm."

"HI, LINN!! CHEER *UPPPPP*!" he roared in my ear, like the dork he was.

"*Billy!*" I reprimanded. "Shut up and listen, 'cause I can't stay on long. How come you didn't get back to my text yesterday?"

"Well . . . 'cause I felt a bit funny about what you called me, Ally."

"What?" I frowned, aware that Linn was tapping her manicured fingernail on her watch. "What did I call you?"

"*You* know."

"No . . . I don't know! What are you on about?"

"You said—"

"Hey, Ally! ALLY!!" yelled Sol at surprisingly close range. "Are you trying to *remind* me of something, sitting like that?"

"Huh?" I said, thrown by Sol's remark. I mean, I was hunched on the coolbox – so what?

In my ear, I could faintly hear Billy saying my name and sounding confused, but Sol was right in front of me, bellowing some more and drowning Billy out.

"Still, at least you're not half-undressed today! Ha, ha, ha!"

Omigod. I suppose I *was* sitting with my feet sprawled and knees together, just like I had been on the loo when he and Lana had walked in on me.

My brain seized up, as I registered shame and shock: shame at Sol's naff comments and shock that Rowan had slapped her hands over her mouth in a failed attempt to hide her giggles.

"Uh, who was that?" asked the voice in my ear.

"Sol. His name's Sol," I told Billy hurriedly, throwing an I'd-like-to-kill-you-now look Sol's way.

"Oh. OK. I – well, I'd, um, better go. Bye."

"Billy?" I said too late.

He'd already hung up.

I took the phone from my ear and stared at it, trying to figure out what he must be thinking.

"Ally . . . you can phone Billy back, if you want," Linn said gently, putting her watch down on her towel.

With that simple, kind offer, I knew that she knew that we *both* knew how very, very, horribly bad that all must've sounded to Billy.

Suddenly, I wished I'd had the good sense to push *Sol* in front of that speeding ice-cream van earlier. . .

Chapter 8

RED NOSE DAY

One kind deed deserves another. Unfortunately, I was slightly allergic to kind deeds.

Mum's kind deed of this afternoon had been twice as bad as I'd expected, thanks to Sol saying what he did (Linn's mobile was currently in my lap, and I was desperately willing it to ring or bleep, hoping Billy would reply to one of the six texts and voicemail messages I'd left for him). And now that Daniel had invited us for Sunday tea to say thank you for taking care of his kids, I had a horrible feeling that something bad was going to happen; that I'd end up embarrassing myself and my family by losing control, jumping up from the table and strangling Sol with a tea towel. . .

"I guess it's just the problem with being a farmer," Daniel was saying to Mum and Dad. "When I was working our place in Yorkshire, I never saw enough of my kids. And since my marriage broke up and I bought this place here to be closer to my sister . . . well, much as I love Sol and Lana coming to visit, the cows still need to be milked and the chores still need to be done, day in, day out!"

"It's not exactly a nine-to-five job," Mum commiserated, looking fondly from Daniel to Val and back again.

What a history they all had together. . .

"Oh, Ivy, Ivy, Ivy – I've missed our cuddles *so* much!" said Val, kissing the top of our little sister's head.

Ivy just giggled and then wriggled herself off Val's knee, galumphing off around the big farmhouse kitchen in her wellies, in hot pursuit of four dogs and Tor. Yes, I did mean to say four: Rolf, Winslet and Ben had a new best buddy in Arthur, the elderly collie, who'd come as part of the fixtures and fittings when Daniel had bought the farm. Luckily for Arthur, who was a bit creaky and wheezy round the edges, Daniel hadn't wanted to keep sheep, so Arthur's only duties around the place were to sleep a lot and wag his tail in a pleasing manner.

"Dad! Do they *have* to!" said Lana, standing still with a large bowl of salad clutched in her arms while a flurry of fur and chasing kids flew around her.

From the expression on her face, you'd think she

was trying to wade through a sewage pipe. My dogs and my little brother and sister weren't *toxic*. (Just, er, too *bouncy*.)

"Sit down, relax, and ignore them, Lana," said Daniel good-naturedly, taking the bowl from his daughter and pulling out a chair for her to sit down on.

"Yeah, just shut up, Lana, you moaning old bag!" Sol chipped in.

Hmmm . . . which did I like least? Snotty Lana, or rude Sol? I think Sol still won hands down. He just opened his mouth and let the cheekiest, rudest rubbish dribble right out, and no one seemed to stop him. Even his dad just rolled his eyes and joined back in with the general conversation round the table.

"So the shop's not doing too great at the moment, then?" Mum was asking Val.

"Too much competition, I guess!" Val shrugged, tearing at a bit of bread.

We'd stumbled on Val's shop last year, when we'd come looking for Mum. Seabird Ceramics was one of about a zillion craft shops peppering the tiny, windy roads and lanes of St Ives.

"You need a USP," Linn suddenly said, without glancing up from carefully buttering her bread.

It was the first time she'd spoken all evening.

She'd been in such shock when she'd glanced in her make-up mirror earlier and seen the tomato glow of her nose (*not* a good look for a perfectionist) that we'd assumed she'd lost the power of speech. Before we'd come up here to Daniel's, she'd spent twenty minutes trying to cover her nose with concealer, but it hadn't brightened her mood.

"Huh? What's a USP supposed to be!?" sniggered Sol, with that mixture of a sneer and grin on his face that I'd already – in such a short space of time – grown to know and loathe.

"Unique Selling Point," Lana added flatly, as she examined her knife and didn't look too impressed with its cleanliness. "We did it in Business Studies."

Linn glanced up at her and nodded. "You've got to find something different to sell, Val. Something no one else has."

"Maybe you could sell *these*!" said Rowan, holding up the, er, thing that was dangling from her neck. "I made it myself the other night! I was thinking of getting a stall and selling stuff like this . . . sometime in the future, I mean!"

Whoops, Rowan had almost let slip about her non-excellent idea to do with Brighton. Still, she didn't seem too upset about her abandoned plans and her split with Alfie at the moment. She'd even gone overboard and "dressed" for dinner tonight, pulling out a long, maroon slip dress from her suitcase, and a staggering range of accessories (belly-dance coin belt, a flurry of life-size butterfly hairclips, a tinkling silver anklet, charity shop beaded bag and the, er, thing dangling from a rose-red velvet ribbon round her neck).

"What is that supposed to be anyway?" asked Sol, leaning closer for a look at the circular neck-thing Rowan was holding up for all to admire.

"It's a dreamcatcher," Rowan said, blinking down at her artwork with pride.

"What? Like those stupid New Age spiderwebs?"

That was Sol, in case you hadn't guessed.

"They're not spiderwebs!" Rowan laughed lightly, choosing not to hear the sarcasm in Sol's voice. "American Indians used to use them to hang in tepees and catch bad dreams in the night!"

Sol's "Yeah, *right!*" was drowned out by a frenzied bout of barking and some shrieks as the kids and dogs all dived under the table and out again, making the plates and cutlery rattle.

"And what's that in the middle of your dreamcatcher?" asked Daniel, pointing at a blue-ish blob in the middle of the criss-crossing silver lines within the circle.

"It's a bruised heart," said Rowan, a little wistfully. "It represents a bad dream of mine. . . But I thought I could customize them for people; ask them what their nightmares are and put whatever it is on their own personal dreamcatcher necklace!"

I'd never have said it out loud in a million years, but Rowan's necklace looked more like the sort of string and glue muddle that Ivy would trip home from nursery with, rather than something that could be displayed in a shop window. Mum was beaming though, proud of Love child number two following in her own artistic footsteps. (Um, to give you a feel of my mum's style of art, you may be interested to know that she just did a kids' workshop in papier mâché *clothes*. . .)

"Ah, it's lovely, Rowan," Val lied, "but I don't have much luck selling necklaces, as there are a couple of handmade jewellery shops on either side of me. . ."

Suddenly, the sound of Beyonce's "Crazy In Love" trilled from my lap. There it was on the display – Billy's mobile number.

"It's for me!" I told Linn, in case she thought it was one of her friends.

I swivelled round in my chair, for a tiny sliver of privacy.

"Hey, you!" I said, in as quiet a voice as I could manage.

"Woah!" yelled a voice close to me. "Check it *out*! Looking *gorgeous* there, baby!"

Sticking a finger in one ear, I glanced round to see who Sol was bellowing at. It was Linn, who'd blown her nose, accidentally wiping some concealer off and exposing her tomato nose to the world – and Sol's ridicule.

"Is that that Sol guy again?" said Billy.

On one of the voicemail messages I'd left, I'd waffled on and explained who Sol was, why he was hanging out with us, and the fact that he'd caught me in a compromising position in the shack-of-a-hut-of-a-loo.

"Yeah, but. . ."

"He seems to like you. Gorgeous, eh? That's nice. Um . . . listen, someone's calling me – I've got to go."

And he was gone. Gone with the thought in his head that Sol's yelled remark was a) genuine and not sarky, and b) a compliment aimed at *me*, and not an insult to Linn and her nose.

I stared down at the phone, trying to remember how to do call-back, instead of keying his whole number in again and wasting time.

But I didn't get the chance.

"Can I have the phone, please, Ally?" Linn ordered rather than asked, grabbing it from my hands as she stood up. "Excuse me – I forgot that I promised to give one of my friends a call."

And off she stomped, to give Nadia or Mary or both an update on the hideousness of her holiday, while I sat still and stunned, knowing that Billy had the wrong idea bouncing about in his brain.

"Pssst!"

I wasn't sure where the pssst! noise was coming from. I glanced over at the Aga (a vast cooker the size of a tank), to check if Daniel had left a pot or pan on.

Nope.

"Psssst!"

I'd seen Daniel slot an ancient cassette into an equally ancient tape player on the worktop when we'd arrived. Maybe the cassette had finished and was making a "pssst!" noise as it rewound, like our old video machine at home did.

Nope – above the general chit-chat, dog and kid noise, there was still the soft voice of some woman warbling away a sixties-sounding song.

"Pssst!"

Now *this* "pssst!" was different; it came with an accompanying tug on my trouser leg. I lifted my eyes to check that everyone was back to chatting and eating, before bending over and peeking under the table.

I was practically nose-to-nose with both Ivy and Tor.

"Winslet is doing a bad thing. . ." whispered Ivy, her brown eyes wide with her bad thing secret.

"I tried to make her stop," said Tor, his face full of worry.

In the gloom and muddle of table and people legs, I could make out one brown, furry pooch, hunkered down in that worrying pose of concentration that Winslet does when she's eating something she shouldn't be. At home, that could mean toothbrushes, socks, homework and remote controls. This evening, it meant one of the expensive trainers that Sol had kicked off.

"We'll have to tell, won't we?" whispered Ivy.

"Leave it to me; just you go and find the other dogs to play with," I told my brother and sister reassuringly. "*I'll* stop Winslet."

Or maybe I won't, I added in my head, as Tor and Ivy scuttled off and I sat up and silently went on eating my tea.

Ah, revenge is sweet (and chewy). . .

Chapter 9

A BAD CASE OF SQUASHING

What do you get when you mix a sneer with a grin? There should be a word for it. A snegrin, maybe. Or a greer.

Sol's snegrin or greer had been horribly *leering* into my face, when I suddenly flipped wide awake.

What a horrible dream.

Maybe I needed one of Rowan's wonky dreamcatcher necklaces. I wouldn't want her to make a miniature of Sol's face to stick in the middle of it, though – I couldn't stand looking at even a tiny, looky-likey version of him. Maybe she could do a cockroach instead – yeah, that would represent him pretty well. (No offence to cockroaches.)

I decided I'd ask Ro in the morning, along with another question I'd been dying to quiz her with once we were on her own; i.e. why exactly she seemed to think it was fun to hang out with Sol. . .

I had planned on running that by her last night,

in the privacy of our tent, but thanks to my sleep-free session the night before, I'd zzzzzzzz'd off long before she'd tootled back from a torch-lit trip to the shack-of-a-hut-of-a-loo.

But hold on; why had I woken up now? It was still dark, and I was still tired. Maybe it was something to do with the fact that I couldn't move my legs . . . or my arms. And I was very hot.

Is this what a stroke feels like? I wondered in a panic.

Luckily, I could still lift my head.

And luckily – thanks to a bit of moonlight – I saw that I *hadn't* had a stroke; I was just suffering from a bad case of squashing. Two-man tents just aren't made for four Love children, three dogs and assorted lions and tigers and teddy bears. . .

"Tor," I said softly, spotting my brother stir as he tried to lift Rolf's leg off his head.

"Hnnnuh?" he muttered back, blinking in the semi-darkness.

"Tor, why are you all in here?" I whispered, pulling a trapped arm out from underneath a teddy-snuggling Ben.

"Ghosts. . ." mumbled Tor, sitting up now and rubbing his eyes.

"Ghosts? What, you had a dream about *ghosts*?" Tor and his soft toys often found their way up to my attic bedroom at home after nightmares. Looked like he'd just swapped the comfort-zone bedroom for a comfort-zone tent, just 'cause *I* was in it. It was very sweet, really.

"'Snot a dream," he yawned. "The big tent's haunted."

I swept a pile of soft somethings and a hairy tail to one side so I could bend over and put an arm around him. At the same time, my elbow nudged over the empty milk carton I'd been using as a vase for the droopy, dried-out carnations Billy had given me.

"Uh, Tor . . . I think it's pretty rare for a tent to be haunted. Like in, I've never heard of that happening ever before."

"But it *is*!" he insisted, just loud enough to make Rowan start to stir. "I heard all this whooshing, and heavy breathing. . ."

"It wasn't just Dad or one of the dogs snoring, was it?"

"I know all the sounds that all the pets make!" he said, slightly indignantly. "And Dad goes '*arrrrrghhh-arrrrgh-ruuuup!*' when he snores, not '*whoooooosh, whoooooooosh!*'"

Tor was pretty agitated, as you could tell from the fact that he was talking a lot (for him).

"What's whooshing?" murmured Rowan, trying to elbow her way upright, and earning a growl from Winslet for disturbing her. "And why are you all in here?"

"Tor says the big tent is haunted," I explained.

"Haunted? What're Mum and Dad saying about that, then?" said Rowan, making a tinkling racket as she lazily scratched her head (how could she sleep wearing all those bangles?).

"Wait a minute; they don't know you're here, do they?" I sussed out.

"Didn't want to wake them. . ."

As Tor spoke, Rowan sighed and wriggled her way out of the sleeping bag and out of the tent with some seamless pushing and nudging of sleepy bodies. After a second's thought, the three dogs all followed her, hoping for an early breakfast. Fat chance; I knew she was off to shake our parents awake and tell them of the night's tent-swapping shenanigans.

"Honest, Tor, I really don't think it could have been a ghost," I tried to reassure him. "It was maybe the wind in the trees, or some of the things Rowan has stuck on this tent making a racket."

"Trees and stuff on tents don't *breathe*," he told me, not in the mood to be reassured.

"What about a fox, then? Maybe a fox was out for a walk, and came sniffing around the tent. That would be cool, wouldn't it?"

Appealing to Tor's animal-fixated mind; that could work.

"Why would a fox go *'whoosh-whooosh'*?" he quizzed me.

My mind went blank, apart from a stupid image of a fox outside, playing with a toy spaceship made out of a washing-up liquid bottle and some silver foil...

"Hey, guys!" said Mum, appearing at the entrance of the tent. "How about I grab Ivy, and we all go back to the big tent for a chat and a snuggle, hmm?"

"Don't want to. Want to stay here," said Tor, slipping his legs into Ro's still-warm sleeping bag.

Mum looked at the snoozling Ivy, took on board what Tor had just said, and came up with an alternative suggestion. "Do you want to go sleep in the big tent, Ally, and I'll bunk in here tonight with these two? Rowan's already getting comfy over there..."

And so five minutes and some whispered chat with Dad and Rowan later, I found myself trying to get comfy in a Clifford the Big Red Dog bed that was made for someone less than half my size.

And five minutes after *that*, I heard nothing but the rhythmic breathing of Ro and Dad, as they fell asleep, untroubled by ghostly figments of Tor's imagination.

I closed my eyes, cuddled Mr Penguin (who'd somehow got left behind in the exodus) and tried to get cosy. Well, OK, my knees were cosy, since that was about all the Clifford blanket covered.

Here it came, that lovely, sleepy feeling, sloshing softly around me like a puddle of syrup. Any second now, I'd be zzzzzzzzz-ing off, hopefully dreaming dreams without a snegrin or a greer in them. . .

Whooosh-whooooosh!

I sat up ramrod straight, thought I heard a shuffle and a snuffle . . . and then silence.

I squeezed Mr Penguin so hard that he was in danger of losing his stuffing, and listened some more. Still silence.

Had I dreamt up Tor's ghost in that funny, hazy place between sleeping and waking? Or had there really been a whoosh of haunting going on?

"*Arrrrrghhh-arrrrgh-ruuuup. . .!!*" Dad suddenly snored.

Well, that racket was sure to scare ghosts away, I decided, lying back down.

Now I just needed to think of some happy thoughts to get me to sleep.

HobNobs. . .

Colin the cat. . .

The first *Lilo and Stitch* movie. . .

Ice cream, all kinds. . .

When Mum came home for good. . .

Ivy. . .

Tor hanging upside down from the stairs, doing his bat impression. . .

Nachos. . .

All crisps (except for those special edition Marmite ones – yeuchh!). . .

New trainers. . .

Favourite *old* trainers. . .

Hanging out with Kyra (except when she's being annoying). . .

Grandma's cooking (mmmmm). . .

Watching laser beams whirl into the sky from my bedroom window whenever there's a big show or concert on at Alexandra Palace. . .

Did I say crisps. . .?

Billy, goofing around. . .

Oh, Billy.

There wasn't anything I wanted more right now than to hear one of his corny jokes, or – better still – have him say something soppy and sweet to me.

Even if he did want to say it in the cartoon voice of a sea slug. . .

Chapter 10

THE HAPPINESS HEAD-COUNT

"Wow, this is *soooo* beautiful!" gasped Rowan, holding a large crystal prism up to catch the sunlight streaming through Val's shop window.

Ro was seeing the world through rainbows of colour. With one normal and one weirdly magnified huge eye, if you were looking at my sister and the crystal from where I was standing.

Watching her (funny) face all lit up with wonder, a dumb thought popped in – without asking – to my head.

Hands up who's happy. . .?

If I'd said that to my family last Friday, everyone's hands would have been up – except for Linn's (of *course*).

If I'd asked them on Saturday, Rowan's arms would have been flopping at her sides, same as Linn's.

And so today was Monday. And if I shouted "Who's happy?" now, who would be reaching skyward?

Mum, for sure: she was having a ball catching up with old best friends (like Val and Daniel) and old general friends (like half of St Ives).

Dad would probably have his hand up. Although he'd been a bit quiet today: he'd been doing a lot of smiling and less talking, which if you know Dad isn't totally like him.

Rowan. Well, it definitely looked like *she* was happy, from the grinning and giggling she was doing yesterday with Sol. And she was in her artistic element, as we hung out in Val's deserted craft shop this morning.

So that was the happiness head-count. What about the rest of us? Well, in the not-so-happy camp there was Linn (hey, no surprises there), Tor and Ivy (slightly rattled and ratty today 'cause of ghosts and disturbed sleep), and me (fretting over what was going through my dumb, lovely boyfriend's mind right now).

I'd quite liked to have chatted to Mum about it. About Billy getting the wrong end of the stick, about Sol waving the stick around in the first place (so to speak) and how Billy hadn't answered any of the messages I'd left for him.

Or Dad would have been good to chat to as well, for a "you-were-a-teenage-boy-once" insight into what Billy might be thinking.

But like I said before, it didn't happen very often; getting either of my parents on their own, I mean.

Though sometimes at home, when Dad was taking a turn bathing Tor and Ivy (i.e. getting soaked by them), and Rowan was doing her homework (i.e. daydreaming about being Johnny Depp's stylist in his new movie, with her French book open in front of her), and Linn was at one of her friends' for tea (i.e. comparing straighteners and planning her escape to Edinburgh), I might catch Mum all by herself in the kitchen.

And then we'd pull up a cat and have a chat about life, the universe and everything. Or maybe just about how painful it is to get a spot on your eyebrow, for some reason. Or how it's scientifically impossible to paint your toenails a dark colour without smudging. Stuff like that. And then, of course, she might ask me how things were going with Billy, and I could say fine, and make her laugh by telling her how he'd skateboarded into a bollard or got chased by a Canada goose at the ponds after deliberately eating the last bit of stale bread I'd brought to feed the ducks with.

So today, yeah, I'd have loved to get her on her own, but I was currently sharing her with my sisters and Val, while Dad stayed back at camp to play in the brook with Tor, Ivy and the dogs.

"The *second* tent is haunted?" Val frowned at Mum, while me and Rowan bumbled around the customer-free shop, looking idly at crystal prisms, nautical mobiles, seagull-patterned teapots and shell-shaped loo roll holders.

"That's what Tor said." Mum shrugged, taking a sip of peppermint tea. "We were both snuggling down to sleep beside Ivy last night, when he insisted that he could hear the whooshing sound. I couldn't make anything out, but it took hours and about a hundred whispered nursery rhymes to get them both to calm down and nod off, finally."

"He better not think about dragging Ivy and the dogs into *my* tent tonight," Linn grumbled, as she texted her mates with one hand and went through her bag of emergency shopping (hair wax, hair serum, hairspray, hairband, value pack of babywipes and a lock she was going to ask Dad to fit on the shack-of-a-hut-of-a-loo door) with the other.

"Hey, I just thought: Daniel's got a spare room at the farmhouse!" said Val. "It's not much bigger than the bed that's in it, but you and the little guys could stay there tonight, just so they get a good night's sleep!"

"Oh, but I couldn't," Mum started to protest. "Daniel—"

"—won't mind a bit. I'll call him right now," Val insisted, already dialling a number into her shop phone.

"Well, maybe it *would* be an idea, just for *one* night," Mum mumbled.

My heart pinged at the sight of it . . . the phone I mean, not Mum's face. The thing was, I *had* to talk to Billy. And if he wouldn't answer his mobile, then I'd call his home phone. And I could do it right now, in privacy and for as long as I wanted – depending on how much money I had in my pocket.

"Back in a sec," I told Mum, pointing at the phone box just across the street, though I knew she was too distracted with Val and Daniel's phone call to listen to me properly.

Linn glanced up, but Rowan didn't: she was busy checking out coasters made of dried seaweed.

Great; I had a big handful of change, I realized, as I stepped out into the windy, shop-lined lane. If Billy's in, I can have a proper chat with—

"SOL!" I shrieked, as the front wheel of a bike and a dementedly grinning lad came hurtling deliberately towards me. . .

* * *

Sol wasn't grinning any more. From the bench I was sitting on, Sol looked miserable, like he was a cool six-year-old boy who'd just been coerced by his teacher into playing a soppy lamb in the Nativity play.

It was probably because he wasn't really an art gallery and museum kind of person. We were at the Barbara Hepworth museum right now, which is basically the house and garden of an artist called Barbara Hepworth (duh!) that got turned into a museum when she died. Mum, bubbling over with enthusiasm, was currently trying to help Sol appreciate the sculptures dotted around the gardens. But the more she cheerfully chattered on about "touchable forms" and "nature in abstract", the more miserable Sol looked.

Hurrah!

Apart from being pleased to see him look uncomfortable (served him right for scaring me to death earlier), I was also pleased to notice the puncture marks in his left trainer, thanks to Winslet's chewing session on it during tea last night.

"Check it out – I got a postcard of this one," said Rowan, suddenly sitting down beside me on the bench. She held out – at arm's length – a card with a photo of a big, marble stone with a hole in it, so that in our eye line, it was right beside the *real* big, marble stone with the hole in it.

"Uh-huh," I nodded, tilting my head to the side to try and see something in the sculptures to make me like them as much as Mum and Rowan obviously did.

"You know I was thinking. . ."

Oh, dear, I sighed to myself. Just as well Linn had gone to find the loo; whenever she hears Rowan say those fateful words, she can never stop herself from groaning.

". . .about something to help give Val's shop an edge. Y'know – like Linn said last night, a UPS."

"USP," I corrected her. Since UPS was a worldwide parcel delivery service, Val would probably only need them if she got a sudden bulk order for driftwood napkin rings from Siberia or somewhere.

"Yeah, that," Rowan nodded, making the butterfly clips fastening the ends of her tiny plaits clatter together. "I think she needs to come up with, like, a St Ives mascot to sell!"

"OK. . ." I said warily, taken aback by the fact that Rowan's idea sounded quite good.

"So I was thinking, maybe Val should make and sell mini versions of these sculptures!"

"But . . . but the artist Barbara Hepworth did

these," I pointed out, looking around the small but busy museum garden. "So wouldn't all her stuff be copyrighted, or whatever you call it when you can't nick an idea?"

"Ohhh. . ." mumbled Rowan, deflated. "Right."

"But a mascot's a good idea!" I said, trying to brighten her up again.

"Yeah, I'll have another think. Hmm, and maybe right now I should go and rescue Sol – I think Mum's maybe overloading him with information."

As soon as she stood up, I pulled her back down by the hem of her tie-dyed T-shirt.

"Wait a minute, Ro. I wanted to ask you something; how come you invited Sol along today?"

That's what Sol had told me earlier, after he'd screeched his brakes and stopped his bike a cat's whisker-breadth away from smashing me in the kneecaps.

("Rowan said you were all going to one of those lah-di-dah galleries in town," he'd snegrinned at me, "and said I should come too, if I was bored. So I got bored, so I'm here.")

Rowan sat back down beside me, shoving her postcard into her bag.

"Um, I dunno . . . I just thought it would be fun to invite him along, 'cause he's a laugh!"

"What – he's a laugh 'cause he stuck his head through one of those holes in the stones and got told off by the security guard?" I pointed out. "Or that he started imitating that bunch of American tourists in the gallery really loudly?" (*"Omigahhhdd! These rawks are soooo awesome!"*)

"Well, y'know," Rowan answered uselessly.

"No, I don't know. Why don't you explain? I mean, how come you seem to like him so much?"

"'Cause he's kind of loud and silly, I s'pose," Rowan attempted to answer.

Yeah, but he was loud and silly in a *bad* way, unlike Billy, who was loud and silly in a *good* way.

"And I guess he's just, I dunno, helping take my mind off Alfie and all that stuff. . ."

So she was still thinking about her ex, sort of.

"Are you sorry that you chucked Alfie now?" I asked, more gently.

"No! Specially since he doesn't care. I mean, he hasn't even tried *once* to contact me to say sorry!"

Er, what exactly was Alfie supposed to say sorry for? Being the only one with a brain between the two of them? And another thing. . .

"Rowan – we're on *holiday*. How is Alfie *meant* to contact you?"

"He could . . . he could always call me on Linn's mobile!" she insisted.

"But, Ro, you said you don't want Linn to know what's going on!"

"Exactly!" she exclaimed, making precisely no sense at all. As usual.

Thank goodness for Linn wandering back over. She might be a grouch, but at least she was sane.

"Ally – text for you from you-know-who," she said, handing me her mobile.

My eyes scanned the message, my heart was in my mouth. But all it said was, "*Hey, it's me – is that you?*" Still, I liked it. A lot. It sounded short and stupid and typically Billy, so at least he was still talking to me.

I could vaguely make out Mum's voice, asking Linn to help her choose a postcard in the gift shop for Grandma, but that didn't really filter through the replies I was running through in my head. Till Mum called to me, and motioned me over.

Now the *sensible* thing would have been to keep hold of the mobile while I went to see what Mum wanted. But instead, I did a really *not-at-all-sensible* thing; I passed it to Rowan and said, "Can you hold this a second?"

What a difference a second (or ten) can make.

Mum had called me over to solve a dispute; getting a postcard for Grandma was just a ruse, as she was keen to buy a book about Barbara

Hepworth for Rowan and keep it for her as a Christmas present. Linn was humming and hawing, saying that although Ro seemed keen on the place, Barbara Hepworth's sculptures weren't really sparkly enough to be a real hit with Ro. I had to agree with Linn; Mum would be better giving Rowan the money and setting her loose in the haberdashery section of a department store for ten minutes. Rows of ribbons and sequins would be Rowan's idea of heaven.

Ten seconds over, it was time to reply to Billy's text.

Except the mobile – and my sister – weren't where I'd left them. . .

And then I spotted a flash of tie-dye, partially hidden behind a bunch of tourists.

"Don't!" I heard Rowan say, in that half-pleading, half-giggling voice you use when someone's torturing you with tickles.

But Ro wasn't being tickled – she was trying to grab Linn's phone back from Sol.

"Awww . . . cute message from your boyfriend, Ally!" Sol snegrinned at me. " '*Is that you?*' "

"Give that to me," I said, trying to sound stern, and knowing I probably didn't.

"But I'm just trying to help – thought I'd answer his question for you!"

Have you ever seen a wide smile that didn't mean anything nice? I hadn't till I looked at Sol's face right then. My heart lurched, as much as my hand did towards the mobile. But again, he held it just out of reach. I had to try another tactic, and act like I didn't care, even though I really, really did.

"*Wrong number. Get lost. Durrrrr!*" read the message on the screen.

"*Very* funny," I tried to say drily.

"Yeah? You think so?" said Sol, widening his eyes at me. "Well, this is even *funnier*!!"

And blam – Sol hit the "send" button, just like that.

It was all I could do to stop myself from hitting *him*. . .

Chapter 11

AN INTESTING ADVENTURE!

Reasons why it was tricky to get in touch with my boyfriend:

1) It's difficult to phone from a field, due to a lack of phone boxes. (I guess cows don't tend to call each other too often.)

2) It's hard to get a bit of privacy when you're surrounded by the entire Love clan, barking dogs and VIPs (Very Irritating People, i.e. Sol and Lana).

3) It's tricky when your boyfriend isn't answering his messages, and thinks you've a) called him a name you can't remember, b) you're hanging out with another boy, and c) have been texting him rude messages.

4) It's difficult when your only regular means of contact is through your sister's mobile, when the battery for it has run down, and there's nowhere to plug the charger in. (Yep, cows don't have electric sockets in their fields either.)

Number four, at least, was solved for now; Linn was up bright and early this morning, and headed to the farmhouse to take up Daniel's offer of a shower (she'd got fed up of trying to wash in a basin of lukewarm water) and charge her phone. She felt brave enough to do it today, I guess, since Mum and Tor and Ivy were all there, having spent the night in Daniel's spare room.

Yep, Mum had taken up Val's suggestion/ Daniel's offer of a sleepover at the farmhouse with the kids (even though I'd overheard Dad telling her earlier in the evening that she was overreacting and that he thought it was a pretty duff idea). To me, it had been really, truly, *severely* weird, lying in the festooned tent last night beside Rowan, knowing that half our family was sleeping somewhere else. It must have been weirder still for Dad, who'd been all alone in the family tent – with three snoring dogs keeping him company, of course.

Anyway, speaking of weird, it was also goosebumpy weird to keep being introduced to people in the street who knew Mum from before (before she came back home). I mean, these strangers were clued into a whole chunk of Mum's life that *none* of us – Dad, me and my sisters and brother – had ever been part of. . .

"This is going to be an intesting adventure!" said Ivy, gazing out of the gospel bus window at the greenery whizzing by.

We'd all been a bit quiet, lost in our own, varied thoughts, as Dad steered the minibus along endlessly windy lanes in search of the dog-friendly beach Daniel had told us about. But Ivy's earnest, mispronounced, little comment got us all smiling, and aware of each other again. (Perhaps not Sol; he had his headphones on and blaring too much to join in.)

"It certainly will be!" Dad said, smiling at Ivy in the rear-view mirror. "Hey, instead of building a snowman, why don't we build a sandman?"

"Or a sand*ghost*!!" Tor said breathlessly.

Uh-oh. A night in a non-whooshing room hadn't exactly rid Tor of his haunting fixation quite yet. Of course, I hadn't mentioned my own, sleepy-dreamy, imagined whooshing of two nights ago, and I wasn't about to bring *that* up in front of impressionable eight-year-old boys right now.

"Well, maybe. . ." Dad answered Tor dubiously. "Speaking of ghosts, your sisters and I didn't hear anything last night, did we girls?"

Me, Linn and Rowan gave a quick, enthusiastic chorus of "no!"s.

"So I think any ghosts that might have been around have gone away now," Dad continued. "Which means you and the toys can all sleep in the cosy big tent again tonight!"

"No, thank you!" said Tor matter-of-factly, while Ivy clutched Mr Penguin tightly and shook her bobbed head.

I saw Mum and Dad shoot looks at each other, the sort of shorthand glances that meant, "What are we going to do?" and "I don't know!"

In that microsecond exchange, they must have come to the decision to tackle the problem later, 'cause next thing, Mum was chirpily changing the subject. Or maybe Mum had just decided to change the subject herself, since Dad suddenly looked on the grumpy side of bemused.

"Pity Lana had a cold and couldn't make it."

Mum's comment coincided with a track ending on Sol's iPod, which unfortunately made him chip in with our conversation.

"Nah – she's just using that as an excuse," scoffed Sol. "She didn't want to come!"

How rude. The last thing Linn wanted to do today was climb in the chug-a-lugging, exhaust-smoke-puttering gospel bus, but she was still here, sitting beside me and flicking a fake smile on to her face whenever Mum or Dad looked round. So why couldn't Lana make the effort, since my mum had been nice enough to invite her? Not that I particularly missed Lana's company. I appreciated the fact that she didn't seem quite as obnoxious as her brother, but since she didn't bother trying to talk to anyone in my family except for Mum (who, it had to be said, was the one starting the conversations), she wasn't any great loss.

But one thing was funny about Lana. . . I got this flutter of déjà vu every time I looked at her, but just couldn't figure out why. Maybe she was a little bit like my friend Salma, who was cool and aloof and gorgeous – but then Salma was three years younger and quite a bit shorter, while in the hair and skin department, Salma was brown and olive, while Lana was blonde-ish and pale. So who *did* Lana remind me of? Someone else at school? Or maybe even someone off the telly? If my poor, frazzled mind wasn't whirling like a dervish (whatever one of *those* were), maybe I could figure it out.

"Oh! Oh, well. . ." Mum said dubiously, in reply to what Sol had just come out with. "Never mind. I'm sure we'll all have fun. Or as Ivy said, we'll have ourselves an 'intesting' adven—"

KKKKKRRRRRRROOOOOOOIIIIINNNNN GGGGG!!!

"Eeeeee!!" shrieked Rowan and Ivy in unison.

"%@£x!!!" swore Sol.

"What's that?" I asked stupidly, as if anyone could say for sure what that terrible, crunching/screaming noise was.

KER-junk, KER-junk, KER-junk, KER-junk...
went the gospel bus, as it thundered and lurched to a stop by the side of the lane.

"Well, I'm no car mechanic," said my dad (who was a bike mechanic), "but I think it's safe to say we've broken down..."

Oh, yes, we'd broken down. In the middle of nowhere. With a herd of vaguely curious cows chewing grass and staring at us over a fence.

It took Dad five minutes of noseying in, out and under the minibus to come up with an explanation.

"I've got no idea," he muttered, scratching his head.

"So what do we do?" asked Linn.

"I'll keep checking. And in the meantime, we could always *pray* for some help!" Dad grinned, tapping the name on the side of the bus.

Linn shuddered, instinctively imagining us all being stranded here in this isolated spot for days, without access to hot running water or hair serum.

"Should we flag down a car for help?" I suggested.

"Yeah, *that'll* be right! Seen any lately?" Sol snegrinned at me.

Still, the little weasel was right. We hadn't seen a car – or a house – in the last half-hour.

"Look, it's fine!" said Mum breezily, for the sake of Tor, Ivy and Rowan, who all looked on the verge of whimpering. "We'll phone Val on Linn's mobile, and she'll get a garage to come out and help us!"

There you go – it was that simple. One quick call and we'd just have to pass the time by making daisy chains or shoving Sol into cowpats before help arrived.

Or that *might* have been the plan, if Linn's mobile had worked. . .

"Fine! Plan two is *this*. . ." said Mum, after seventy-five attempts (up the lane, down the lane, in the field, etc.) to get reception, and failing. "*Dad* carries on trying to fix the minibus, while *we* all have a walk *this* way, and try to find a phone. On the map, there's a little hamlet just before you get to the beach."

The flaw in Mum's plan was that a fretting Tor and Ivy didn't want to go, and wouldn't let Mum go either, leaving me, Linn, Rowan, Sol and three excitable dogs to trudge our way hopefully towards a phone and help.

It took three minutes of trudging, till we'd turned a corner in the road and were out of earshot of Mum and Dad, for Sol to start acting up.

"Heard back from your boyfriend, then, Ally?"

I didn't need to look at him to guess the expression on his face.

And I didn't need a mirror to know I was going bright red with anger, humiliation and frustration. If only I had a fairy godmother, I'd wish that she'd give me some witty, crushing put-downs I could spit Sol's way. Or maybe I could just wish for my mate Kyra to be instantly ker-powed here; she's got such a sharp tongue she'd cut him into a million boy pieces.

Well, to be realistic, there was no way Kyra could wade in for me, but I was forgetting what Linn could be like when she was riled.

"You want to give it a rest, Sol?" she growled low, like a she-lion who wasn't to be messed with.

"Get *over* it!" laughed Sol, ignoring the warning signs. "That message thing was just a joke! Right, Ro?"

"Um, well, yeah . . . but maybe you shouldn't have actually *sent* it. . ." said Rowan, wimping out as she was caught between loyalty to me, who she'd known for fourteen years, and this new buddy, who she'd known for just over two days.

"Yeah?" nodded Linn, walking hard and fast, as if she was imagining it was Sol's head she was tramping on. "Well, it's not much of a 'joke', if you get your kicks from upsetting people, is it?"

It would have been nice to hear something along the lines of, "Oh, I never thought of it like that", but Sol wasn't a sorry-I-see-your-point kind of person. He was one of those yeah-but-I'm-just-being-me people, who think they can get away with saying and doing whatever they like, whenever they want.

"Look, Rudolph, just chill *out*!" he snorted in my big sister's direction.

Linn stopped dead in her spotless white Adidas trainers, her face (and especially her sunburnt nose) glowing red with anger. She turned to glower at Sol, fists on her hips. Even *I* was scared, and she was on my side.

"Listen, Sol, I know your dad and your aunt are friends with our mum," she said, the restrained anger making her voice deeper, "but if you open your mouth *one* more time, I'm going to *ram* something in it."

Instead of shutting up, Sol did the exact opposite, opening his mouth wider and laughing out loud.

"That's *crazy*!" he sniggered, when he could get his breath back. "That's *exactly* what my sister says to me!!"

Before Linn could reach for her trainer/a nearby stone/anything else that came to hand to pelt him with, Rowan piped up with an important piece of information.

"Look! Over there – a petrol station!"

More importantly, it was an old-fashioned looking petrol station, with a rescue truck parked at the side of it.

"I'll go and talk to someone inside," muttered Linn, turning away from the irritation of Sol now that she had something worthwhile to do.

"Great! Do they sell stuff? I could murder a Mars bar!" said Sol, trotting after her, unbothered and unscathed.

That left me and Rowan, but I wasn't really in the mood to chit-chat with her, since she hadn't exactly done a great, sisterly job of being an ally to me.

And then I spotted something almost as exciting as stumbling on the lone petrol station: a phone box.

"Got to make a call," I mumbled, rifling for change, and hurrying away from Rowan and hopefully towards reconciliation with Billy, if I was lucky.

"Hello?"

"Mrs Stevenson? It's Ally!" I said, my heart pounding with relief. The last couple of times I'd called, I'd just got the answering machine, or Billy's moody big sister Beth, who was about as reliable at passing on messages as one of our stick insects.

"Ally! How're things? How's the holiday going?"

"Uh, fine!" I lied, since mentioning that her son was in a huff with me, I was being forced to spend time with an obnoxious weasel, and we were currently stranded in a broken-down minibus would've been too much of a headache to go into. "Is Billy there?"

"Yes, of course! He'll be so pleased to hear from you. He'd kill me for saying it, but he's been moping a lot the last couple of days! Hold on and I'll go get him. . ."

Didn't sound like Billy had told his mum why *exactly* he was moping. But then the chances of a fourteen-year-old boy chatting about feelings with his mother were probably about as remote as Winslet winning a doggy obedience competition. (I could see Winslet now, crouching down to wee beside some bags of kindling, completely ignoring Rowan's pleas to come away.)

"Uh . . . Ally," said Mrs Stevenson, coming back on to the phone after aeons of seconds later. "Sorry – I got it wrong. I thought he was in his room, but he must've gone out."

The tone of her voice was trying to sound convincing, but I wasn't. Convinced, I mean. I had a horrible, instinctive gut feeling that Billy was actually hovering near his mum, waving his arms and desperately mouthing "I'm not here!" at her.

I wanted to say something, but the words were bunching up behind a croak in my throat.

"Can I take a message for you, Ally?"

Mrs Stevenson's voice made me so homesick for Billy, I suddenly felt like crying.

In a panic, my brain flailed around, trying to locate *something* to say. Unfortunately, even *I* was surprised by what came out.

"*SOL!!*"

"What's that, Ally? Did you say '*Sol*'?"

Of course, Mrs Stevenson couldn't see what had just scared the pants of me: a leering, dribbling, squished-up, squashed-up face, pressed up against a panel of glass.

And of course, if Billy was standing as close to his mum as I suspected, hearing Sol's name again was going to fill him with joy (not).

Seemed like Sol's latest prank had just got me into a whole heap *more* trouble with my boyfriend.

Gee, *thanks*, Sol.

How could I ever repay him? Maybe by training Winslet to wee on *him* next. . .

Chapter 12

THINGS'LL LOOK BETTER IN THE MORNING (MAYBE)

With the minibus in hospital – probably receiving the last rites – there was nothing to power the fairy lights around the middle-sized tent.

And with Mum gone – to sleep at the farmhouse with the kids *again* – Dad didn't seem in the mood to light any more than a couple of the painted jam jar tea lights, as the daylight started to fade to dusk.

Thanks to Linn's migraine – caused by general holiday stress – Dad hadn't put on the radio either.

All-in-all, the campsite didn't exactly have the quirky party vibe of our first night.

"Here, boys. . ." Dad clucked at the dogs, alerting them to the fact that there was a lot of leftovers languishing on his paper plate. He hadn't eaten very much. Neither had Linn, who'd picked at some salad before announcing she was off to her tent for a lie-down. Rowan hadn't eaten with us at all; some time after the rescue truck had dropped us back here, she'd borrowed Lana's bike and cycled into St Ives with Sol, with plans involving a chip shop along the way.

And now. . . Well, with only the sound of the small fire crackling and the slurp of a dog or three, I decided to make the most of something I moaned about not having very often: a parent to myself.

I glanced over at Dad. He was wearing his favourite pair of straight-leg jeans (which looked identical to all his other straight-leg jeans), and a vintage '50s short-sleeved shirt with a pattern of a cowboy lassoing stuff (his best holiday shirt). He looked lost in thought, probably frazzling his brain over how he was going to tell his mate Neil that the gospel bus had died on us.

"Mum knows so many people here, doesn't she?" I said, just to get the conversation started. It even turned out she knew the bloke who drove the rescue pick-up – Mum had bought Ben as a puppy from his sister.

"Yep, she sure does," Dad muttered, tossing a twig on to the fire and watching it sizzle.

I was about to witter something else, something nice about Daniel and Val, which might lead me on to moaning about Sol, when Dad said something else, something so quiet I almost didn't quite catch it.

"Seeing Melanie so happy, it makes me wonder

if she ever regrets it. . ." he said, softly and sadly.

"Regrets what?" I asked him.

I suddenly felt shivery and chilly, despite the warm air and cheery fire. Mainly because I knew exactly what he meant.

"Coming back to us. Leaving here," he said simply, and paused. "Sorry, Ally Pally – I shouldn't be saying things like this to you. I don't mean to upset you!"

How funny – Dad thought I'd be traumatized, and actually I was pleased. 'Cause in the back of my mind, I'd been wondering the same thing ever since my parents had first announced the holiday plans. And the thought had been wriggling around, unnoticed, even more since we'd been in St Ives and half the population had been waving at her and hugging her like a long-lost relative.

It would be really great to talk about this with Dad, since he was being so honest, and there was no one around to interrupt.

"YAAAYYYYYY!" came a shout from the lane, as two bike lights suddenly twinkled into view.

Our three dogs went mad, hurtling towards the gate. Except I made that four. . . I squinted in the half-light and realized that the slower dog bounding along at the back was Arthur the collie – he must have been out on a night-time walkabout and joined in with our pooches when he saw them lolloping along.

"Hiiiyyyaaa!" trilled Rowan, her voice sounding like one of the tiny bells fastened to our tent in comparison to Sol's bellow.

"Listen," I said to Dad, "can I sleep in the big tent tonight? Since there's more room?"

"Course you can, Ally!" Dad shrugged.

"Good, 'cause I fancy an early night."

Dad looked a bit surprised as I grabbed one of the jam jar tea lights and zoomed-at-the-speed-of-very-fast-light towards the family tent. But all he did was nod his head of spiky brown hair in my direction and said nothing more than, "Night, night, then, Ally Pally – sweet dreams."

Once inside the tent, I wriggled into Mum's sleeping bag just as I was. My baggy shorts and T-shirt would do for pyjamas tonight – I wasn't going to leave here to get my grotty jim-jams from the other tent, and find myself having to chat to the dreaded Sol, who was yakking some nonsense outside to my dad right now.

Instead, I stuffed a bunch of tissue in my ears, stared at the photos of all the pets taped to the inside of the tent, and tried to think nice, calming thoughts before I blew the tea light out.

Then, like a charm in the dark, Grandma's voice

seemed to talk some sense to me – in a muffled way, of course, thanks to the tissue in my ears.

"Everything will look better in the morning," I thought I could hear Grandma say soothingly.

I blew a kiss to the photo of Britney the cooing pigeon and blew out the candle.

Yep, tomorrow was a whole new day. A better day. A day that (thanks to going to bed way too early) was a whole, calming, thirteen hours' snoozles away. . .

Five hours later. . .

"*Urghhhhh! Naaaaaaahhhhhhhh!*"

Even in my not-quite-awake state, I knew that the urghhhh-ing and naaaaahhhh-ing was coming from somewhere outside. Had Tor's ghost got fed up with *whoosh-whooshing* and heavy breathing? Was it trying to spook us in a new and exciting way?

A scramble of activity from the sleeping bag at the other side of the tent meant Dad had heard the whatever-it-was too. So had Winslet, Rolf and Ben, who were all sitting up, ears aloft, muzzles pointed at the entrance to the tent.

"Stay there, Ally Pally!" said Dad, scrambling out of the tent in his Clash T-shirt and boxer shorts, a torch in his hand, followed by three protective furballs.

Yikes – Dad was obviously out there checking that Rowan and Linn, in their individual tents, hadn't been attacked by ghosts or mountain lions or prehistoric dinosaurs on the loose.

I needed to cuddle something, badly. But without a spare dog or a Colin the cat, or a cat-that-wasn't-Colin, all I could do was reach for the first Blu-tacked photo to hand. Oh, yes, in the name of comfort, I'd ended up snuggling a photo of Flapjack the speckly brown rat. Nice.

Then above the sound of my heart *ba*-boom, *ba*-boom, *ba*-booming, I could hear voices. It sounded like Dad and Linn talking fast, and possibly panicky, but I couldn't make out what they were saying exactly, thanks to the rain I now realized was hammering down on the tent, like the heavens had opened and spilt tons of frozen peas down on us.

"Arrrrgggghhhh!!" growled Linn, launching herself into the big tent so suddenly and alarming me so much that Flapjack the rat suffered un-repairable scrunching.

"What?" I mumbled, thinking I'd never seen my sister look so . . . so . . . *rough*. Course, the way she was holding the torch in her arms, along with a bundle of clothes and bags, was doing her no favours. (Try holding a torch under your chin in the dark, and check yourself in the mirror – you'll give yourself nightmares.)

But it wasn't just the unflattering torchlight; Linn was soggy and ruffled, her hair a tangle of curly, wet wisps. She looked like she'd been dragged through several hedges front, side and backwards.

"I was having a nightmare that I was drowning," she explained, chucking her armful of a bundle on to the ground, and wiping wet tendrils away from her face. "And then I woke up soaking, 'cause of the rain pouring in a hole in the tent, right above my head! *Oof* – Rolf! *Must* you?!"

A muddy-pawed Rolf apologized for barging his way in by licking Linn's face. She *loved* that (ha!). Winslet and Ben didn't bother apologizing, they simply barged in with a gruff growl hello (Winslet) and a dopey doggy smile (Ben), before whirling themselves round into a comfy snooze spot.

"Where's Dad?" I asked.

"He's taken my sleeping bag into Rowan's tent – it's still dry-ish. He's going to stay there tonight, since I've got all my stuff in here. Rowan's still zonked out – can you believe someone can sleep through a rainstorm this loud?"

Or your yelling, Linn, I thought to myself.

She shone the torch over the damp, jumbled

piles of clothes (and the steaming, sleeping dogs). For a neat freak, this was like a vision of hell. Linn was coping remarkably well.

Then again, maybe not.

"Oh, Ally!" she said, suddenly dropping her face into one hand in abject misery.

I shuffled over as fast as my knees would take me and put my arm around her.

"Things'll look better in the morning," I said, hoping my Grandma-ism would hit the right spot.

"*How?*" Linn mumbled. "My nose will still be burnt. We'll still be on this stupid holiday. We'll still be cramped together in these horrible tents. We'll still have to wee in that shack. . ."

"I know you're hating it, but we've only got Wednesday, Thursday and Friday, and on Saturday, we'll be driving home."

Maybe. If the gospel bus made a miraculous recovery.

"Yeah, and my exam results will be waiting for me, and if I don't get the grades. . ."

I wasn't going to say, "Of *course* you'll get your grades!", in case I jinxed it for her, or in case Linn's brain had seized up when she'd sat her exams and she'd answered all her science questions in French or something.

"Try not to think about it," I said instead, pretty lamely.

"And what should I think about instead?" she asked, lifting her head to look at me, though she probably couldn't see much since the torch was currently illuminating Winslet's bum. "Should I think about what an idiot Rowan's being, and how quickly she's managed to get over Alfie?"

"What do you mean, get over. . .?"

That sounded suspiciously like she knew.

"Look, I know," she said.

"How? Alfie wasn't meant to tell you – Rowan made him promise!" I hissed, though Rowan wasn't likely to hear, since she was sound asleep and the rain was still battering down noisily.

"He was upset! And who do you talk to when you're upset? Your best friend! Not that I particularly wanted to listen to stuff about my sister . . . specially the stuff about him wanting to get back together with her."

"He does?!"

"Uh-huh. He wants me to pass on a message to her, saying he's sorry if he upset her, and can they talk. I just haven't passed it on yet, because Ro's bugging me too much. As long as she's giggling and acting all flirty with that stupid Sol boy, I'm not doing a thing to help get her and Alfie back together."

Sol; what a guy. Whether he knew it or not, he was a one-boy, relationship-wrecking machine, making trouble for me and Billy, and keeping Rowan and Alfie apart.

Me and Linn sat in silence for a second, before letting out a joint sigh . . . which might have made us laugh, if we'd been in the right mood. Only we weren't, specially since at that exact moment, a loud drip-drip-drip sound caught our attention.

"Oh, *no*. . ." grumbled Linn, shining the torch on the steady stream of rainwater trickling through the roof of the tent.

That saying of Grandma's – about things looking better in the morning. Well, I really hoped it was true, or I just might sue. . .

Chapter 13

SPOT THE COSMIC TWINS

Outside was sunny and bright, as if the weather was trying to fool us into thinking we'd dreamt up the rainstorm last night.

But we had proof. Piles of it. Piles of it coming out of Daniel's washing machine and piles going into his dryer.

"Wonder where he keeps his iron?" said Linn, gazing in a promising-looking cupboard that turned out to have nothing but dog food and wellies in it.

(Arthur the elderly collie opened a hopeful eye at the creak of the cupboard door, and closed it as soon as the door was shut again.)

My eldest sister was looking a lot more like herself this morning, thanks to a long, hot shower and a hair-straightening session. And her mood was brighter, since she was doing something she loved; tidying and organizing. There was a lot to tidy and organize; last night we'd gathered up as much Love family clothes as we could at the drier side of the leaking tent, but there was still plenty that got wet and yucky. Only my clothes and Rowan's had been spared, since they were in the non-leaking two-man tent.

But I'd been pleased to come here and help Linn, since it meant a hot shower (mmmm) and hot, buttered toast (thank you, Daniel). Mum and Dad, meanwhile, were down at the muddy camp, trying to mend tents and sort out the mess, while the dogs and the kids goofed around in the mud.

And Rowan? She'd begged off helping us out, and begged instead to go and help Val: she said she'd had an idea of a way to boost Val's shop; it had come in a vision in the night (apparently).

"What, like an angel?" Linn had said sarcastically, thinking (I think) that Rowan was just using arty-farty-ness as an excuse to skive off.

"Well, a *kind* of angel," Rowan answered, missing the sarcasm altogether and going dreamy-eyed. "But I'm going to keep it a secret, till I see if Val likes the idea!"

Of course, Mum hadn't minded at all, so Rowan had skedaddled off down the lane, while we'd headed up it, with armfuls of laundry.

"The iron's in there, if that's what you're looking for," said a bored-sounding voice, which happened to belong to the girl in the doorway.

Lana was wearing pink striped pyjama bottoms and a vest top, both of which looked just out of the packet, rather than something she'd tossed around in all night. Her hair was sleek and straight, instead of the wayward mop I always end up with when I've just staggered out of bed. She was yawning too, and magically looked quite graceful and not like a double-chinned walrus at all. How was that possible?

I felt that flurry of déjà vu whirl around my memory banks again, and whirl away *just* before I could work out why Lana seemed so familiar. . .

"Thanks," said Linn, pulling open the cupboard Lana had pointed to. "Your dad said we could use your washing machine and everything. We had a bit of a disaster last night—"

"Yeah, the storm. Dad told me what happened before he left for work this morning. Want a coffee?"

"Yes, please!" Linn nodded.

"Er, yes, please," I added, though I noticed that the conversation just seemed to be going on between the two older girls. "The campsite's a bit of a—"

"I was lying listening to the rain last night, and cringing at the idea of being stuck in a tent!" Lana carried on talking directly to Linn.

I was used to this. Linn's friends Mary and Nadia talked over me *all* the time. Older teenage girls have tons of time for each other, and pay plenty of attention to little kids (it's the cute factor), but if you're between nine and fifteen, forget it: it's like you don't exist. Unless you're in their face doing something dumb, which I *was*, of course, that first Saturday night. But since giving Lana a laugh during the shack-of-a-hut-of-a-loo incident, I'd become invisible to her.

"Tell me about it! It's bad enough camping without getting half-drowned too!" said Linn, plugging in the iron.

"How can you stand it? Camping, I mean? I'd go crazy if I couldn't hang my clothes up, or have space to lay out all my make-up and hair stuff! Milk, by the way?"

"Just milk, no sugar, thanks. I know exactly what you mean, I—"

"Hi, Ally! What're you doing here? Stalking me?" Sol said loudly, swaggering into the kitchen in his low-slung long shorts and nothing else.

He was a weasel. An absolute weasel. And yet again, I wished upon wish upon *wish* that Kyra could be zapped here and say something that would have this weasel-boy whimpering.

"Oh, hi, Rudolph! Didn't know you were here

too!" he sniggered, seeing Linn by the ironing board. (Sol *had* to be thick – throwing insults within throwing distance of someone holding an iron is just madness.)

"Sol – get out *now*," said Lana firmly.

"Yeah? How're you going to make me?" Sol dared her.

"Easy. I'll tell them about the time you had to go to hospital because you got your trouser zip caught on your—"

"I'm gone! I'm gone!" said Sol, with the second "I'm gone!" taking place from behind the kitchen door that he'd just closed.

"Sounds painful," Linn smirked.

"It was," Lana smirked back. "I mean, I felt sorry for him at the time, but he drives me so insane sometimes that I'll always be grateful to that zip for giving me the ammunition to shut him up."

"Does he drive you seriously crazy, then?" asked Linn, taking a sip of her coffee.

(Like a last minute thought, Lana threw another coffee together and handed it to me without looking my way.)

"Crazy? There are times when I'd love to wake up and find out that having a brother was just a bad nightmare and not real at all!"

"God, I know what you mean. My sister Rowan *completely* does my head in. She's such a ditz! At home, I just have to get away from her and all the mess in the place and lock myself in my room."

"*That's* how I feel here! Have you *seen* the way my dad lives?" exclaimed Lana, coming to life as she pointed to a drooped, unwatered plant on the windowsill – one of many round the house, I'd noticed. "I know he's working, working, working all the time, but it's just so *scuzzy*. . ."

BLAM!!

Luckily, that *wasn't* the sound of Sol charging back in, with another barrage of barbed comments aimed at me and "Rudolph". Instead, it was the sound of a big, fat realization hitting me in the face.

BLAM!!

Actually, make that two.

Realization number one was that for the first time in ooh, *such* a long time, Linn was looking happy and animated.

Realization number two was that it was because she'd found a neatness-obsessed, control-freak soulmate. Lana and Linn were the Cosmic Twins of Grouch!

"And speaking about my dad – you know the

worst thing he did to me?" Lana was saying. "When I was born, he only went and persuaded my mum to call me after the city they went to on honeymoon!"

("Lana"? Was that the capital city of Namibia or somewhere?)

"No *way*! My parents did nearly *exactly* the same thing to me!" Linn gasped at the coincidence. "But go on – you tell first!"

"Atlanta, that's my proper name. As in Atlanta, Georgia. I mean, couldn't they even have named me *Georgia*? At least it's a real girl's name! But no, they go all hippie-fied and land me with Atlanta, and all I can shorten it to is Lana, which I still end up having to explain to *everyone*. . ."

Just before Linn launched into her Loch Linnhe saga, a thought popped into my head.

"Lana, can I use your phone for a second?" I asked cheekily.

As soon as Lana nodded, I shot out of the door, checked that Sol was out of sight and earshot, and dialled a number.

No – not Billy's (again), but Kyra's.

'Cause watching Linn and Lana there reminded me that everyone needs a friend now and then.

"Yeah?" Kyra's bored voice answered, making my heart soar with hope.

"Kyra, it's Ally – you've got to help me."

"Shoot," said Kyra, in that infuriatingly casual voice of hers.

Wow, it felt good to talk to her. . .

Chapter 14

NOT A GOOD PING

Q: How many Love children and dogs can you fit in a phone box?

A: Three (Love children) and one (dog).

In this particular phone box in Hayle, just along the coast from St Ives, the squashees consisted of me, Tor, Ivy and Arthur the collie, who was sitting on my trainers and panting happily.

And what were we four humans and a dog doing in a phone box in Hayle?

To answer the phone box bit first, it was Wednesday afternoon and Tor was putting in a mid-holiday call to Grandma to check on the welfare of the pets. (I'd called Kyra for an update, but there was no answer – I'd just have to wait till she got in touch with me as promised tonight on Linn's phone.)

The Hayle bit, well, the good news was that a garage here had been able to fix the gospel bus, and we were here to collect it.

"Did she make a 'pppttttttttt' noise or a 'rrrrrrrr' noise when you did it?"

Tor was currently asking Grandma how Peppa the guinea pig had responded to Grandma tickling her tummy, as he'd instructed (pet rule No. 214, probably). Since I knew that Grandma had no intention of doing anything except *feeding* the pets, I wasn't sure how she was going to answer. . .

"She went 'pppttttttt'?" said Tor happily. "*That's* good – it means she's happy!"

(Grandma must be relieved that she guessed the right answer.)

"Uh-huh. . ."

Tor shoved the phone towards me. A boy of very little words, he didn't feel it was necessary to explain that Grandma had just asked to speak to me.

"Grandma?"

"Hello, Ally, dear. How's everything after the storm?"

"You know about that?" I asked in surprise, wondering if my very sensible and down-to-earth grandmother had suddenly turned psychic.

"Linn told me. She's been calling me every day with all your news."

Every now and then (like in the dripping tent last night), I get a ripple of love for Linn. It's those rare glimpses of the normal girl, with normal feelings, behind the Grouch Queen façade. And I felt a ripple for her now, knowing that she'd been phoning Grandma for a chat, and not just sitting around growling to herself about her hair straightening woes.

"Well, the big tent's fixed, but Linn's is totally wrecked," I told Grandma, thinking about the soggy, torn paper chains and flooded fairy lights that had had to be dumped along with the one-man tent. (The campsite was looking pretty plain and dull now.)

"So where's everyone going to sleep?"

"Mum and Tor and Ivy are already staying at the farmhouse. . ."

"*And* all the toys!" Ivy chipped in, jumping up and down and nearly standing on Arthur's tail in her wellies.

". . .*and* all the toys," I added for Ivy's benefit. "And now Daniel's daughter Lana has asked Linn if she wants to come and sleep on the floor in her room tonight."

Over laundry, coffee, moans about names and families this morning, Lana and Linn had totally bonded. They were even off on a girlie shopping trip to St Ives this afternoon.

"I see. And how's Rowan? Linn said she's made a new friend. . ."

"Kind of," I answered, gazing out of a glass pane

at the sight of Sol thudding a tennis ball noisily against the outside wall of the garage. "But she's busy today – she's helping Mum's friend Val in her shop, I think."

Val had left a message with Daniel, saying that Rowan had come up with a fantastic idea for a St Ives mascot, and if it was OK with Mum and Dad, they'd be working on it in the shop today. I hadn't been too thrilled to hear that; while Rowan was acting as Sol's playmate, it kept the weasel out of my face, for *some* of the time at least. As it was, on the drive here in Daniel's Landrover today, I'd had to put up with Sol sitting beside me, singing rude songs (just loud enough so only *I* could hear), and nudging me hard with his elbow, right before each sweary word. Lovely.

"And what's happening with the minibus, Ally, dear?"

"It's fixed – we're here to pick it up from the garage. I think Mum's just paying the repair guy."

As I talked to Grandma, I could see Mum, standing in the large open doorway of the garage, waiting for the bill to be sorted out. She looked young and pretty and carefree, as she and Daniel laughed at something he'd just said.

Something in that easy, comfortable laugh made my heart go *ping!*, but not in a good way. I thought of the cut-short conversation with Dad last night, about Mum being so happy here in Cornwall. I thought of his smile-free face this lunchtime, when it was decided that he'd stay behind and do more camp-fixing with the dogs, while Mum would take up Daniel's offer of a lift to Hayle.

And when the Landrover – packed with all of us – drove off, he'd looked so forlorn as he waved that I'd felt like shouting for Daniel to stop and ordering Mum out of the car to go give Dad a hug immediately.

But of course I didn't. Instead I just waved back at him, though I don't know if Dad saw, 'cause Arthur was sitting in between me and the door, his hairy head hanging out the window, tongue lolling happily.

"And how are things with *you*, Ally?" Grandma asked now. "Linn was saying you've been having a bit of boy trouble."

By that, did Grandma mean Billy? Or Sol? Or both? Whatever, it would be *soooooo* good to talk to her. Grandma was exactly the cool, calm, rational person you needed to moan to when you had a twisty head. And I still had sixty pence of talk-time left.

"Well—"

"Me! Me! I want to speak to Grandma, please!

Pleeeeaaasseee, Ally! Please-please-please!!"

How can you turn down a small pink person with pleading brown eyes?

"Ivy wants to say hello first," I explained, handing the receiver down into her hands.

"Got wellies – they're pink! Sort of. They've got pink bits! And I can jump in the mud and the dogs jump too, but they haven't got wellies, but that's OK because they're dogs and dogs don't have wellies and—"

As Ivy prattled on, I saw Mum wave to the mechanic and then wave her keys at us – it was time to go.

"Tell Grandma the bus is fixed and we have to say bye," I told Ivy.

"The bus is fixed and I have to say bye-bye!" blurted Ivy, immediately going up on her tiptoes and practically throwing the receiver back in place, cutting off the call.

So there'd be no helpful chat with Grandma for now. Just the weird sight of Mum giving another man (i.e. Daniel) a kiss on the cheek before they went to their own vehicles. . .

"See you back at the field, Arthur!" Tor called after the elderly dog, as it lolloped off at the sound of Daniel's whistle to come.

Going back to camp in our separate ways might

be disappointing – from a doggy point of view – to Tor, but it had its advantages. For one thing, it meant I didn't have to watch Mum and Daniel getting on *way* too well, and it also meant I didn't have to be within annoyance distance of Sol.

But he wasn't out of annoyance distance quite *yet*.

"Hey, Ally – catch!" yelled Sol, giving me next-to-no warning, as his tennis ball already flew fast and hard towards me. *That* was going to hurt. (Sol's intention, maybe?)

But not if I took a step *this* way. . .

A whirl of yellow whizzed safely by me, and was last seen bouncing its way into the busy, main road traffic.

I shrugged casually in Sol's (stunned) direction, grabbed Tor and a pink person in each hand and headed towards the gospel bus.

Well, look at that. Some of Grandma's cool, calm rational, er, *ness* seemed to have rubbed off on me. . .

Chapter 15

WHEN A FAVOUR ISN'T A FAVOUR AT ALL

Looking round the restaurant table at my family, I could see an "us and them" situation arising.

The "us"s (me, Dad and Rowan) looked like we'd been up all night herding sheep in a blizzard. The "them"s (Mum, Linn, Tor and Ivy) looked fresh as newly washed daisies. What a difference an overnight stay and a shower in a comfortable farmhouse can make. . .

"There!"

Tor, sitting next to me, had been concentrating very hard on cutting his round pizza into some kind of a shape.

"That's nice. What's it supposed to be?" I asked.

"An antelope, of course!" he said, glancing up at me with a frown.

"Antelpope," Ivy backed him up, the red tomato sauce around her mouth clashing with the three pink serviettes she'd shoved into the neck of her pink top.

Yeah, an antelope; any fool could see that.

Except *this* fool, who'd thought Tor's latest food art was maybe a fork-lift truck or a crane or something. (Oops.)

Speaking of pizza, the pepper and sweetcorn (with extra sweetcorn) one in front of me smelled just *mmmmmm* . . . if I'd been in the mood to eat, that is. My stomach might well have been sending urgent messages to my brain, complaining of being on starvation rations, but my brain was too busy fretting to notice.

Today's reason for fretting? A day and a half, and Kyra *still* hadn't called me back (don't even *ask* about Billy).

I was trying to make up excuses for her (and him). I mean, it *was* possible that an asteroid had hit Crouch End, and the news just hadn't filtered down here to Cornwall. Right. . .?

Boink!

I winced as another tiny, paper airplane crashed into my forehead. It was the third since we'd arrived here. In the circumstances, Grandma's cool, calm rational-ness was starting to wear off fast. . .

"Sol, your aunt's only just had those leaflets printed up, so *please* don't waste them!" Daniel scolded Sol, slapping his hand on the pile of paper, and pulling it away.

I unfolded the latest plane that had just boinged

into my forehead, and read the message: *Swoop to Seabird Ceramics, for the one souvenir you can't leave for home without!* The style of the lettering was modern and bright, and the simple, airstream-gliding seagull illustration was very classy (obviously Rowan had nothing to do with the leaflets, then).

It was Thursday evening – our second last night in St Ives – and we were all gathered together in a pizza place, having tea. Val and Rowan had joined us straight from the shop, where they'd been working hard on their secret project.

Yep, while I'd spent thirty-six hours waiting impatiently for contact from home, Rowan had virtually vanished from the family unit, doing her mysterious arty-crafty thing with Val.

And other things that had happened in the last thirty-six hours? Well, there'd been paddling and sandcastles and ice cream, but they were all a vague blur compared to the panic in my heart that I might not have a boyfriend when I got home.

"Hey, Martin!" Val said to my dad, leaning over the table conspiratorially.

Was she finally going to let us in on Rowan's amazing mascot idea?

"Uh-huh," said Dad, dragging his gaze away from Mum, who'd spent the last five minutes at the kitchen door, chatting to the owners of the restaurant, who she'd known from her previous St Ives life.

"Daniel's had a great idea," Val continued. "He thought we could have a bit of a party—"

"—at the shop tomorrow night," Dad came in. "Yes, Melanie told me. She said you'd planned to have a bit of a do to celebrate . . . whatever it is you and Rowan have come up with."

When the shop closed at six, there was going to be drinks and nibbles and hurrahs at the grand unveiling of . . . whatever it was, which would go in the window, ready for first thing Saturday morning.

"Well, yes," Val shrugged. "But as quite a few of our friends are coming to the launch party anyway, Daniel had this excellent idea to turn it into a double celebration. He's invited lots and lots of Melanie's old friends, so it's a great send-off on her last night!"

"Party!!" Ivy squealed gleefully, thudding the toes of her wellies under the table in excitement.

"Shhh!" Daniel smiled at her. "We've got to keep this a secret, Ivy. It's a surprise party for Mummy!"

"Yay!!" whispered Ivy, clutching her fists to her chest and smiling the biggest smile.

I could see Dad trying to get a smile together, but it wasn't really working.

"Can the dogs come?" asked Tor.

"Sorry, no, honey," said Val. "They might knock stuff over with their tails. They'll have to stay up at the farmhouse with Arthur, like they are tonight."

Tor looked crestfallen. If anyone had given him the choice, he'd have probably opted to stay in the farmhouse with the pooches instead of hanging out at the pizza place with us. Actually, the mood *I* was in, I'd probably have felt the same, if it wasn't for the fact that I wanted to stay as close to Linn and her mobile as possible. . .

"Hey, Martin, can you imagine the look on Melanie's face tomorrow night, when everyone turns up?" Daniel grinned at Dad.

"Ha-huh."

That was Dad attempting a casual laugh, I think. It was just as well Val and Daniel didn't know Dad well enough to realize it wasn't anything remotely like his normal, relaxed laugh.

Maybe only *I* knew what he'd been thinking the last few days, but that odd laugh alerted all the Love children to the fact that something was up.

"Are you all right, Dad?" asked Rowan, jangling away as she put her arm out to him.

Linn, Tor and Ivy stared, waiting for a reply.

"Bit too much chilli," said Dad, pointing to his (chilli-free) pizza as a cover-up.

"Well, I think Melanie will *love* you for organizing it!" Val carried on with the original conversation, blasting a beaming smile at her brother.

And I think my father looks like he's just been kicked in the stomach by a bad-tempered donkey, I thought, watching Dad now.

Thinking about Dad; thinking about tomorrow; the jangling music from the speakers; the general hubbub in the restaurant . . . put all that together and it meant that I didn't hear the strains of "Crazy In Love" warbling from the new bag Linn had bought during her shopping trip with Lana today.

"Hello? Oh, hi. Hold on. . ."

My heart stalled, as Linn's phone came towards me. Could it be. . .?

"It's Kyra," said Linn quickly, before I got my hopes up.

"Hi, Kyra."

I kept my fingers crossed that my voice sounded friendly, and not too flat, or too disappointed that it wasn't Billy.

And then I remembered that Kyra was *seriously* late in ringing me back. A whole *day* late, if you were counting. And I was.

"Where've you been? I thought you'd promised to call me back last night?"

"Well, I *would've* done, if I'd managed to get hold of your stupid boyfriend by then."

"And have you spoken to him now?" I asked, swivelling round in my seat, and wondering if anyone would notice me slithering under the table so I could talk in privacy. (Answer: yes, they would – Sol for one was keeping his nosey, weaselly eyes on me.)

"Yep. I went round to his at teatime."

My heart started hammering so loud that I was sure the owners of the restaurant would come over any second and ask me to turn it down.

"How – how was he looking?"

"Like Billy, in a baseball cap! How *else* would he look?" barked Kyra.

"Yeah, but what did *you* say, and what did *he* say?" I persisted, too used to Kyra's blunt way of speaking to take the slightest bit of offence.

"Well, *I* said, 'What's up with you?' and *he* said, 'Nothing'."

Wow, how I hated that "nothing" that means the exact opposite. It's like when people say "it's fine" in that way that means it's most definitely not.

"And I said, 'Well, why are you being a big berk and ignoring Ally?'"

Kyra Davies. If she ever sat a GSCE in Being Subtle, she'd fail it, no problem.

"And *he* said, ''Cause I don't think she likes me so much anymore'–"

I gasped, shocked that the big berk could really, truly think that.

"– and then *I* said, 'Don't be stupid', and then his mum shouted that he had to come 'cause his tea was ready, so then he said 'bye'."

"And that's it?!" I checked with her, hoping she'd add that he'd pulled the door back open at the last minute and told her he was only joking and everything was fine, and he'd be there to welcome me back home on Saturday with the hugest hug in the history of human hugs.

"Yeah, that was it. D'you want me to go and hassle him again tomorrow?"

"No . . . don't bother," I said morosely, thinking there was no point in Kyra listening to more not-so-sweet nothings. "Listen, I better go. . ."

I pressed the button and turned to hand the phone back, interrupting Linn's chat with her new buddy Lana.

"All right?" Linn mouthed at me. (Now, *she* would definitely pass an exam in Being Subtle.)

I just shook my head, and got up, thinking I'd head for the loos, to give me a chance to rearrange my thoughts and my face into something neutral.

But I didn't get as far as the loos. . . Following

the signs, I pushed through one, heavy door, began climbing a flight of stairs, and then stopped at a window half-way up, as a familiar rattling sound yanked at my heartstrings.

Outside, down behind the pizza restaurant, a bunch of skater boys were sitting on a wall, watching as one of their mates came careering down the lane. The boy balancing on the board didn't have a baseball cap on, but he was lanky enough and had dark enough hair to remind me a bit of Billy. Specially now that he'd just tried to jump on to the wall, over shot it and landed in a crumpled pile at the other side. . .

"What's up?"

I didn't want to spoil a beautiful/sad moment by looking into a weaselly face, so at the sudden sound of Sol's voice I kept my forehead firmly on the cool glass of the window and my gaze fixed on the Billy clone.

"So, I said, what's up?"

I didn't have the energy (or brains) to be cool or sharply witty, so I just said the first thing that came into my head.

"Look, I miss my boyfriend. OK?"

I guess I was expecting to hear a sarky "Aww, boo hoo! *Poor* you!!", but instead, Sol said something completely un-weaselly and surprising.

"Why don't you call him then? Here, you can borrow my mobile, if you like. . ."

I was completely thrown. Since when did Sol act nice? It was like a lion sidling up to a zebra and offering it a choc ice, instead of eating it for lunch.

"Go on," he said, holding out the phone, as I turned my head to look in his direction.

"There's no point," I said, wondering to myself if there maybe *was* a point, if anything maybe *had* changed in Billy's head since Kyra had tried to talk to him. "He's not answering."

Sol didn't seem to want to sneer. Maybe he felt genuinely sorry for sending that stupid text on Linn's phone the other day (*and* the *rest*).

"Well, just leave a message. Or text him or something," he urged me.

Wordlessly, I took the phone, and started tap-tapping. "*Hey you . . . still talking to me?*" I wrote, deciding to keep it simple. It had to be worth a try.

"That it done then?" asked Sol, as I pressed "send".

"Yes. Thanks," I replied, handing the phone back to him.

"No worries."

Wow, look at us – talking pretty much nicely to each other. Who'd've guessed?

We both turned and glanced out of the window at the sound of another skateboard (and boarder) hurtling into something solid. I felt suddenly hopeful instead of miserable. Maybe everything wasn't as bad as it had seemed only five minutes ago.

"So . . . wonder what he'll think?" said Sol.

"Huh?"

A bad feeling had just wormed its way into my stomach.

"Your boyfriend!" he replied, snegrinning at me for all he was worth. "He won't recognize the number you've called from. Still, if he gets back to you, I can put him straight, *don't* you worry. . .!"

With that, Sol sauntered off, stuffing his mobile into the front pocket of his jeans.

Omigod. Never mind answer any calls, Sol could also get Billy's number by checking on the message I just sent, and zap off who knew how many cringeworthy/insulting texts to Billy. And there was absolutely nothing I could do about it.

Y'know, it was bizarre if you thought about it; out of all the weird and wonderful hobbies in the world that Sol could've chosen to do, he'd picked being cruel. I wouldn't be surprised if I found out next that he got a kick from tripping up grannies or flicking elastic bands at kittens.

Roll on Saturday, when I'd never have to see the weasel again.

Except I never wanted Saturday to come, because I'd be going home to a boyfriendless, Billy-free zone. . .

Chapter 16

LINN IN HAIR UNFURLING SHOCK...

"Beat the Blues" type articles in magazines; they always tell you to eat some chocolate, or talk to a friend, or hit a pillow or something to feel better.

They might as well tell you to eat a pillow, talk to some chocolate or hit your friend (ouch) for all the good that advice does. 'Cause when you're *really* blue, you don't have the energy to get out of bed, never mind do any eating, talking or hitting...

At least that was the way I was feeling this morning, as my sluggish head throbbed awake, and I could hear the barking of dogs and sound of Dad and Rowan chatting outside.

Like their voices, the smell of veggie sausages and beans cooking on the camp stove wafted in too, but like last night's pizza, I wasn't in the mood to eat. (Sorry, stomach.)

Maybe I could just lie here till we leave tomorrow, I decided. Mum and Dad could just take the tent down around me, and I could crawl into the gospel bus and sit under a blanket till we got home, where

I could lock myself in my attic bedroom till I was twenty-one, or forgot how horrible this week had turned out, whichever came first. . .

And then I was set upon.

"Ouch!" I yelped, as first Tor and then Ivy threw themselves bodily into the tent on top of me, followed by three bouncing dogs and one lolloping dog.

"Yaaaaaaay!" said Ivy breathlessly. "We ran ALL the way down the field from the farmhouse. Play chase with us, Ally!"

"Sorry, Ivy, I'm feeling too tired to – *ow*!"

Ivy, unaware that kneeling on people's boobs isn't much fun, wouldn't take no for an answer. Neither would Tor, who was now physically dragging my legs out of the sleeping bag.

"Got to come play, Ally! Yes, yes, YES! SAY *YESSSSSS*!" Ivy yelled, even though her mouth was exactly half a centimetre from my ear.

"Why are you tired, Ally?" said Tor, now trying to helpfully shove my trainers on my feet. "Did you hear the ghost again?"

"No, I *didn't* hear the ghost, Tor," I told him, realizing I was going to have to give in and get up (though that was hard to do now that a dog had just made itself comfy and settled itself across my thighs).

"Did Arthur come down from the farmhouse with you?" I asked, gently moving the dozy dog and brushing a black and white shedding of hairs off my legs.

"Uh-huh. We came to have breakfast. Mum's on her way too. But not Linn," said Ivy, with a shake of her head, "'cause she's watching boring bands on TV with Lana."

Ah, yes. Eating a croissant off a nice plate, in front of a big telly, versus half-raw, half-burnt veggie sausages on a paper plate on the grass. It was pretty easy to spot which breakfast Linn would go for.

"OK, let's play . . . CHASE!" I yelled, bombing out of the tent before my little brother and sister or any of the bewildered dogs knew what was happening.

For ten minutes we raced around the tents, around the gospel bus, to the shack-of-hut-of-a-loo and back again, with the dogs sometimes chasing *us*, and us sometimes hurtling after *them*.

I was second to collapse (Arthur was first), followed by every one of the dogs and Tor, till only Ivy was standing, panting in her pink swimsuit and wellies.

My chest was heaving and burning as I tried to catch my breath – made all the harder by giggling, thanks to Rolf licking my nose. (Now *this* is something they could put in those "Beat the Blues" features: "Act like a five-year-old or a dog, and run around till you get giddy.")

"Hey, Ally!" Mum laughed, standing over me, the sun halo-ing around her floaty, red-blonde hair. "Need a hand there?"

For that fleeting second, I felt giddy again, with happiness this time. I hadn't had Mum's full attention for days, and seeing her smile beaming directly at me was like coming out of a dark tunnel into a blast of Mediterranean sun.

That was till she helped me up and I saw Sol standing right beside her. *Boy*, I'd like to wipe that snegrin off his face. . .

Had Billy tried to reply to my message? Had Sol sent anything lewd, rude or generally horrible to Billy? I didn't want to give Sol the satisfaction of thinking I was bothered (which of course I was, *desperately*), so I forced myself not to ask him. Instead, I just bent down and patted the nearest dog, which happened to be Arthur. His elderly tail thwack-thwacked gratefully against my bare leg.

"Hey, Sol's got those flyers for Val's shop," Mum said cheerfully. "Are you still up for handing them out in town this morning, Ally?"

Oh, yes, in my haze of misery, at the restaurant

last night – as I sat and fantasized about breaking into Sol's room and nicking his phone while he slept – I remember Val asking if we'd give out those leaflets advertising Seabird Ceramics.

But now my tummy gave a squelch of alarm: last night, I vaguely assumed she was talking to *all* of us. But right now, Mum and Sol were both looking at me, and *only* me. With Linn and Lana bonding over boy bands, Rowan heading down to the craft shop to help out on the project, and Mum and Dad taking the kids to the beach, presumably that meant that everyone was expecting me and Sol to be this happy, little leafleting duo.

I'd rather eat my own *head*. . .

"Ally! *ALLLYYYYYYY!!!*" came a panicked cry from somewhere in the distance.

Several pairs of eyes – human and doggy – swivelled instantly, to see Linn flying down the field in a way that was totally alarming, i.e. her shirt was flapping and her hair was unfurling madly from her tight ponytail.

Something was wrong, *really* wrong.

I started running to meet her, not really caring that I was sometimes stomping through dried-up cowpats.

"What is it?" I called, as loudly as I could manage and run at the same time.

"Hold . . . on. . ." Linn panted, her chest heaving, and her finger pressing the redial on the mobile gripped in her hand. "Here. . ."

As she passed me the phone, she bent over and leant her arms on her legs, trying to get her breath back.

I found myself listening to two rings, then a familiar voice said, "Hello?"

"Grandma?"

What was going on? What would Grandma have to say that was so urgent? And why did she need to speak to only me about it?

"Oh, Ally! Has Linn told you?"

"No, she . . . uh, no!"

I didn't have time to explain. If I didn't find out in the next three seconds what was wrong, I might faint from panic.

"Ally, Billy's Mum just called me. He's gone missing."

In my head, I thought I'd repeated the word "missing?", like a question, but I realized when Grandma spoke again that I'd said a shell-shocked nothing-at-all.

"Ally? Are you there? Have you cut out?"

"*NO!* No – I'm here. What – I mean, how . . . how does she know he's missing?"

I'm an expert at asking stupid questions, I really

am. Presumably the fact that Billy wasn't around had given his mum the idea that he might be missing (duh).

"Mrs Stevenson said she thought he'd just slept in this morning, but when she went to see if he wanted some breakfast, he wasn't there."

"Maybe he just went out?" I suggested, knowing that was almost as stupid as asking how Billy's mum knew he was gone. Billy was a lazy git; he'd never a) willingly get up early in the school holidays, b) leave the house without grunting bye to his mum, or c) go anywhere in the morning without stuffing his lanky self with at least two bowls of Mini Shreddies and four pieces of toast.

"His rucksack was gone, too, dear. And his favourite baseball cap, apparently. Mrs Stevenson's phoned around all his friends, with no luck. You don't have any ideas about where he's got to, do you?"

I had no idea at all. But the reason he'd run off was me; me and that weasel standing back at the campsite. Between us, we'd made Billy so miserable, he'd run off.

Despite the pounding August sun, I'd never felt so Arctic shivery in all my life. . .

Chapter 17

ER, DON'T I KNOW YOU?

"Course this'll be the *second* time it's happened to him," Kyra had commented.

"What – the second time he's gone missing?" I said, trying to get what she was getting at.

"No, the second time he's had a girlfriend go on holiday and hook up with another boy."

Oh . . . she meant Sandie and the school trip. Billy dated my old friend Sandie for a while last year, and hadn't exactly been thrilled when she met Jacob – from one of the other schools on the field trip – and, er, broke up with him (i.e. Billy) straight afterwards.

But even if that's what Kyra meant, it wasn't the same situation now at *all*. . .

"Kyra, I'm *not* interested in Sol, and I'm *not* planning on chucking Billy anytime soon!"

"Yeah, but try telling Billy that," said Kyra. "Well, you *could* try telling him, if you knew where he was, of course. . ."

Talking to my so-called best friend hadn't made

me feel better, in case you hadn't guessed. But then nothing much was going to make me feel better, in the circumstances, as everyone realized.

I mean, no one expected me to go out leafleting after Grandma's news. (A small consolation.) And no one, especially Daniel, minded me using the farm phone to call Billy's mum and Kyra, or parking myself beside it all day in case of any news (there wasn't any).

But even if I felt I was languishing in some weird limbo – where Linn and Lana occasionally appeared to give me drinks and ask if I was all right – life had to go on.

Like for Rowan: she had to hurry up and help at Val's, 'cause if she didn't, the new "mascot" stuff wouldn't be ready for the next day.

Mum – after hovering around with me – took Tor and Ivy away to the beach, as it was the last full day of their holiday and only fair, *and* they were getting kind of nervy looking at my gloomy face.

Dad – after hovering around with me too – had to (slowly) drive the coughing gospel bus back to the garage in Hayle for some fine-tuning, so we'd be able to make our escape tomorrow.

Daniel: well, being a farmer, he had to farm.

And Sol. . . Sol had to go out and advertise his aunt's shop all on his own. Although even in my weird state of limbo I suspected that meant he probably put all the leaflets in the first bin he spotted and spent the rest of the day in record shops.

Then there was another piece of real-life that I couldn't get out of; the half-mascot, half-surprise party at Seabird Ceramics. . .

"Don't forget," Linn said quietly, holding the phone up in her hand for me to see, "I've got it right here."

"And the—"

"Yes, I charged the battery before we left the farmhouse," she reassured me for the twenty-trillionth time.

It was a pity I felt like pants. It would have been a great party if my boyfriend wasn't missing. Oh, and if my dad didn't look sadder and sadder, the more Mum looked happier and happier.

"Ed! Eliza! I can't believe you're all here!" Mum gasped, grabbing the hands of two more people who'd squashed into the packed shop. Daniel stood grinning by her side, almost as if *he* was her partner, and not Dad. I guess Daniel was chuffed that the surprise hadn't been blown yet; that Mum still thought everyone was here to cheer and clap for Val's new business-saving venture.

Speaking of which. . .

"Hi, everyone! Thanks for coming!" Val shouted for everyone's attention, as she turned the music down on the sound system.

The hubbub died away, except for the cawing of two very young seagulls.

"Tor, Ivy – *shhhh*!" I heard Dad quieten them, as he reached out and caught my little brother and sister flapping past him.

"It's lovely to see you all," Val continued, "and it's lovely to introduce you to the youngest artist to exhibit here – sixteen-year-old Rowan Love. Come over here, Rowan!"

I couldn't see much of Ro from the neck down, but from the neck up, she looked amazing. She'd tied her hair into two tight little topknots, and had sewn a mass of pale pink fake flowers on to a headband, with pink and fuchsia ribbons fluttering on either side of her face. Another thicker pink ribbon was wrapped round her neck like a choker. She completely matched the pink balloons outside the shop, the pink fairy lights in the window, and the twirls of shiny, pink tinsel draping from every shelf and surface inside.

My sister had obviously had a big hand in the party decorations, but it did make me worry a bit about the St Ives mascot she'd come up with.

What was pink and reminded people of the seaside? A *jelly*fish?

"Anyway, before I unveil the new town mascot, I just want to say a big thank you to this girl for coming up with something so adorable that I'm sure it's *not* just going to turn around the fortunes of this shop, but give people happy memories of St Ives for years to come!"

An over-the-top, ear-splitting whistle of appreciation came from Sol, making everyone in the place wince, apart from Rowan, who burst into giggles.

Being reminded of Sol's very existence didn't make *me* feel like giggling. *Has he heard from Billy, or said something to Billy?* I fretted in a paranoid way, as everyone else began to cheer and clap for Rowan's sake.

But he couldn't have – hugely irritating as Sol was, he'd have owned up to *something* once he heard that Billy had gone missing. (Wouldn't he?)

Still, right now there was another person I needed to think about. As the clapping and cheering continued, I weaved towards Dad and the kids. Mum was surrounded by a gang of friends, Linn and Lana were hovering together in their cool, cosmic twin way, but Dad looked kind of lost.

"Hi," I said, slipping my hand into his. "How're you doing?"

He gave my hand a squeeze and smiled a grateful smile at me.

"So-so," he answered. "What about you?"

"So-so," I smiled back, just as the clapping settled down and Val got ready to pull a chequered pink-and-white tablecloth off a display behind her and Ro.

"Ladies and gentleman, may I present to you," Val called out, all mock-dramatic, "the mascot of St Ives – IVY!"

And there she was, my littlest sister – or at least a very cute cartoon-y, sculptured version of her – waving in her swimsuit and wellies on the front of mug after mug after mug. Rowan must have worked like crazy, making those tiny Fimo-ish figures, ready for Val to stick on the mugs and fire them in the kiln at the back of the shop. But then all that hard work wasn't the point; the point was, our little sister was *famous*!

"Ivy of St Ives!" read the pink banner above the mugs, and the lettering on the back of the mugs themselves.

"Good grief!" I just made out Dad saying, as Tor went into "It's Ivy! It's Ivy! It's Ivy!" overdrive and the whole crowd turned as one to *awwww* at our sis.

It was all too much for Ivy, who practically scrambled her way up Dad's body and cuddled headfirst into him. I glanced around for Mum, and could just make her out, pushing her way towards us through a sea of smiling, cooing faces.

But she didn't make it all the way over, as Val was currently flapping her arms and urging everyone to be quiet again.

"I think our mascot is a little overwhelmed, but can we perhaps have a few words from her mum? Melanie, can you come over here, please?"

Mum looked torn for a second, but I guess the weight of everyone's expectation got to her. Keeping one eye on Ivy, she made her way to Val's side, as Rowan stepped away. Mum seemed a bit confused by the level of clapping and cheering that had started up again, and was positively taken aback when Val started speaking again.

"Melanie, this isn't just a party for the Ivy mug – it's a party for you too. Because to all your friends here in St Ives, you were very special –" another huge cheer "– and Daniel had the wonderful idea of calling everyone together here tonight so we can let you know how much we all love you and miss you!"

I glanced back at Linn, and then over at Rowan, and our eyes all said the same unsayable thing;

some kind of psychically sent "uh-oh". As for Dad, he seemed to be burrowing his nose into Ivy's hair, but I think it was just a way for him to hide what his face might be showing. I snuck one arm around his waist and gave him a hug, while wrapping the other in a cuddly squeeze around Tor's neck. It's weird to feel suddenly lonely in a room full of happy, laughing people. . .

"Speech!"

"C'mon, Melanie – say something!" came cries from the crowd.

Mum, blushing and twinkly-eyed (and looking all the prettier for it), held up her arms and gave into the demands.

"Well, what a surprise!" she gasped, when at last there was sort-of-silence.

"That was the point!" Daniel shouted over several rows of heads at her.

Mum grinned, and blew him a kiss.

"Thanks for getting this together Daniel, and Val, of course. And thank you all for turning up. I just want to say in return that all the people I met and made friends with in St Ives will always have a huge place in my heart. Being here was a very special time for me –"

Dad moved his head a little, and I could see the threat of tears in his eyes, as Mum said exactly the stuff none of us wanted to hear.

"– because for quite a lot of the time, I wasn't completely myself or completely well," Mum continued. "But your friendships were important to me, and to Ivy. And in your own ways, you all helped me get stronger, until I was ready to find my way home. . ."

I gulped as Mum turned and grabbed Rowan's hand, nodded towards Linn in the crowd, then turned to face Dad, me and the kids.

". . .because home was really where I needed to be, with my beautiful children, and the man I never stopped loving."

I think I'd been in the mood to cry all day, so when Mum said those words and I felt Dad crumple a little, I was off, sobbing so much you could have entered me for the sobbing Olympics. . .

Twenty minutes, lots of tissues and plenty of family (and friends-of-Mum) hugs later and I was feeling a whole lot better.

Maybe I was a little bit drunk-on-happiness, just 'cause I knew for sure that Mum *didn't* regret giving up a world of seagulls, surfboarders and Cornish pasties for us and life in sleepy Crouch End.

That and the fact that I had a *mad* sugar-high,

'cause Tor and Ivy were currently fighting each other to feed me chocolate-covered pink marshmallows from the plate Rowan had left with us. (She'd turned herself into the party waitress, wandering through the glass-clinking, Mum-toasting crowd, offering them the pink nibbles she and Val had decided on.)

"Why were you upset when Mum was talking, Ally?"

I *knew* that was coming. I hadn't wanted to scare Tor and Ivy by crying so much, but I just couldn't help it.

"Ivy, I wasn't crying because I was *sad*," I tried to explain, "but because I was really, really *happy*. What Mum was saying about us all; it made me so happy I . . . uh, cried!"

Tor and Ivy looked at me unconvinced. But then when you're four and eight, the reasons you blub tend to involve falling off your bike or having a big boy push you out of the way at the top of the slide.

"I'm *happy* – honest! Cross my heart and hope to die!" I smiled at them.

"Could've fooled me, the way *you* were going!" growled a horribly familiar, horribly smug voice. "You should've seen the state of your face – your eyes and nose were so red I'll have to start calling you Rudolph too!"

I was *so* not in the mood for Sol, specially with the kids here. He could tease me to the point of driving me crazy when they weren't standing around, staring at us both, but I wasn't having him confuse or upset them.

"Look, we're having a very nice time, so why don't you just—" I really wanted to say something *extremely* rude, but it wasn't exactly the sort of stuff Tor and Ivy needed to hear.

"Just what?" Sol dared me.

"Oh, *forget* it," I sighed, wishing he'd just leave me – and everyone I knew – alone. Except for one person who seemed to have time for him. "Listen, why don't you go and hang out with Rowan? *She* likes you."

"What? Freaky girl with the mad ribbons?" Sol snegrinned, pulling a face and wafting his fingers on either side of his face. "Give me a break! Who wants to hang out with someone who's all 'hee, hee, hee' all the time?"

It was a *horrible* thing to say. It would have been horrible if he'd just said it in front of me, Tor and Ivy, since we were related to her and happened to love her. But it was *especially* bad that he said it when Rowan was right behind him, with a tray of pink, prawn, puff-pastry appetizers in her hands.

I was glad that she tossed them all over him (specially since prawns and puff pastry don't look too good in perfectly waxed fin hairdos), but I was truly sorry that Ro had to hear that.

"Back in a second," I told Tor and Ivy, as I hurried passed a cursing, huffy Sol and through the crowd after Rowan. I saw her darting out of the shop door, but in the midst of the crowd, I felt my arm yanked so hard I had to stop.

"What's he done?" asked Lana, breaking off in her conversation with Linn.

"He said kind of . . . *clunky* things about Ro. And she heard," I explained, instantly realizing that Lana knew that *I* knew we were both talking about Sol. It was the first time in nearly a week that Lana had acknowledged my existence, but I was sort of glad that she was talking to me as another teenage girl for once, instead of pretending I wasn't there, or sniggering at the memory of me in the shack-of-a-hut-of-a-loo.

"Listen, Sol gets everything a bit muddled," said Lana, holding on to my arm pretty tightly. "I know he really likes Rowan, and he really likes you."

Wow. Lana was the only person to know that, then, since I'd always thought Sol *hated* me, for some inexplicable reason. . .

"Could've fooled me," I mumbled.

Lana blinked her perfectly mascara'd eyelashes fast as she seemed to struggle to find an answer.

"Look, I'm not trying to find excuses for him, but Sol was a great little brother until our parents split up. After that, he got angry a lot of the time. And now, whenever he really likes people, he tries to spoil things, maybe 'cause he's used to thinking good things get spoiled. Maybe he'll get better as he gets older. . ."

Lana let the last part of that sentence fade away, as she let go her grip and let me hurry out after Ro.

As I headed towards the shop door, I wondered if Sol *would* become a nicer person in the future. I guessed it could go two ways: would he choose to accept his parents' break-up, or just stick to being sad and bitter and mean for ever. . .?

"Ro?" I said, as I hurtled outside, into the quiet, peaceful lane and the cool evening air.

My sister – in all her party finery – was slouched like a deflating pink balloon on a nearby wall, her tray by her side.

"Don't let Sol bother you," I said (wishing I could have told that to *myself* quite a few times this week).

"I – I – I – thought he was my friend," Rowan hiccuped, said and sobbed all at once (no mean feat).

"He's pretty messed up. Don't worry about what he comes out with," I tried to tell her, after the insight I'd just hoovered up from Lana a few seconds ago.

"But I just feel so – so – so *lousy*!" Ro hiccuped/sobbed some more.

"'Cause of Sol?" I frowned.

"A bit. . ." sniffed Rowan, leaning her head into my shoulder, which was pretty uncomfortable, due to the flower and ribbon festooned headband. "But also because I really miss Alfie too. . ."

What should I say first?

a) that Alfie missed *her*, and she should go talk to Linn about that, or. . .

b) I totally sympathized cause I really missed Billy too.

I decided to settle on point a), since that was the most relevant to Rowan, when my ears pricked up.

It was the sound of distant rattle-rattle-rattling, getting closer and (rattle-rattle-rattling) closer.

Here it came now, in rattle-rattle-rattling close-up; a boy on a skateboard, hurtling round the corner and skidding past us.

Hey – he was the boy from yesterday, who'd reminded me so much of Billy. Except now he had a baseball cap on, which reminded me an awful lot *more* of Billy.

A *lot* more.
Omigod.
It *was* Billy. . .!

Chapter 18

THE PRAWN OF SHAME...

"I got the idea from the athletes."

The party was still going on all around us, but most of the Love family were in the corner, crowded around Billy. Some of my family were even crowding *on* Billy – Ivy was happily perched on his lap, draping strands of pink tinsel around his right ear and trying to feed him chocolate marshmallows off the plate she was holding.

All of us were very, *very* glad to see Billy (me especially, *natch*). Although so far, we were very, *very* confused by his explanation about how he'd got here.

I mean, he'd hurriedly blurted out the main stuff, when I was gawping at him in shock outside. The main stuff was that "everything felt weird all week" (i.e. Billy was jealous), so he'd all of a sudden decided to jump on a train down to St Ives, leaving a note for his parents (not that they seemed to have found one), and look for the one thing he remembered me mentioning ("Seabird . . .

something – I knew that was the name of your mum's friend's shop").

Then – oops! – Billy had had a major freak-out on the train, when it eventually dawned on him how long the journey was going to take. The way he figured, if the shop was closed by the time he got here, and he didn't manage to talk to Val and ask where we were, he'd have been stranded in town for the night with exactly £4.67 in his pocket and a mobile that only had enough charge in it for a one-second phone call.

Once he'd finally got off the train Billy rattled around on his skateboard for a while, till he zoomed down the right road by sheer luck (well, OK, St Ives isn't *that* big), and by *more* sheer luck, Seabird Ceramics was still open, thanks to the party.

Enough of the main stuff, now we wanted details.

"You got the idea from some *athletes*?" I frowned at him.

"*The* Athletes!" Billy repeated, spotting the blank looks on all our faces. "Y'know; the band?"

"Oh, *I* remember ... you've got their first album!" I said, thinking of the teetering piles of CDs on his bedroom floor (next to the teetering pile of magazines, which were next to the teetering pile of clothes he never got round to putting in the laundry basket).

"Um, Billy. . . What's this Athlete band got to do with you being here?" Dad asked. (Mum was on the shop phone at the moment, calling Mrs Stevenson to let her know that Billy wasn't dead in a ditch or anything.)

"Well, I was talking to Alfie in Fab yesterday—"

Fab was a very cool record shop on Crouch End Broadway.

"Alfie? You saw *Alfie* yesterday?" squeaked Rowan.

"Yeah, we'd just bumped into each other and were sort of talking about *mufflemuffle*. . ."

That last bit of Billy's sentence got lost as he went as pink as the marshmallow Ivy was trying to stuff in his mouth.

"Talking about *what*?" I asked him.

"Uh, *you* guys," Billy said uncomfortably, pointing to me and Rowan. I felt myself go a matching pink, whereas Rowan just froze, unsure, I suppose, if Alfie had been saying good things or bad things about her.

"Yeah, *yeah*," Linn burst in impatiently. "But tell us what that band's got to do with you being here, Billy!"

"Well," said Billy, pausing for a second to swallow

the marshmallow practically whole. "In the record shop, they were playing an old Athletes single, really loud. It's called 'Wires', and the lyrics just sort of made me want to . . . uh, come here and . . . uh, see *you*, Ally. . ."

He faded out, looking mortified. And me? Well, now I was just confused again.

"But hold on," I said. "Isn't that song about someone hurrying into a hospital, trying to see their sick, premature baby?"

Boy, Billy's mind worked in weird ways (too many knocks on the head from skateboard accidents, maybe?). What was he on about *this* time?

"Yeah, but it's got this one line in it, something about running, and 'got to get to you'. . ."

Poor Billy. It's all very well to have a big, romantic notion when an indie rock band's playing at full volume, but it's hard to explain a grand gesture like this when you've got tinsel round your right ear and your girlfriend's whole family is staring at you.

"I'll get you a juice, Billy," said Dad, well aware of the embarrassment radiating from my poor boyfriend. As he wandered off, with Tor in tow, Mum's voice drifted over, calling Billy's name. She was holding up the shop phone.

"Uh-oh," mumbled Billy, setting Ivy down on to the floor and walking towards Mum like a condemned man (not that you see many condemned men in films wearing board shorts and tinsel round their ears).

"Mrs Stevenson's going to *kill* him, isn't she?" said Linn.

"Yep," I nodded in reply.

"Oh, but *how* can she be annoyed? It's just such a lovely, lovely, *lovely* thing to have done!" sighed Rowan, all moist-eyed and impractical.

I knew what Ro really meant by that. She *really* meant that she wished Alfie had done something "lovely, lovely, *lovely*" for her too.

But then maybe he *had*. . .

"Er, sorry – completely forgot," said Billy, backtracking a few steps and handing Rowan his mobile. "Check out the last photo – it's from Alfie. I don't know if you'll be able to see it, 'cause I've got virtually zero charge left in my phone. . ."

As Billy headed off (again) towards my waiting mum by the phone, Rowan gingerly pressed the keys, not knowing what she was about to look at, if anything.

"Oh!"

Was that a good "oh", or a bad "oh"? Ah, it was most *definitely* a good "oh". . .

"Look!" Rowan said, dewy-eyed, showing me, Linn and Ivy the image of Alfie holding aloft a soft toy bat, an "I love you" handmade poster and a bunch of purple and pink gerberas. . .

"Pretty daisies," murmured Ivy, standing on her tiptoes to see.

"Awww, isn't that *sweet*?" said a deeply unsweet voice, grabbing Rowan by the wrist and twisting her hand around so he could get a look at the screen of the mobile.

Rowan yanked her arm back, and shot him daggers.

"Are you two all lovey-dovey over your geeky boyfriends, then?"

Sol – he was trying to be . . . well, a bit of a bully. There; I'd got the right word for it at last. And even if Lana had given me an insight into the reason he was like that, I decided that I a) couldn't take it any more, and b) couldn't be bothered with the nastiness either. Same went for Rowan, it seemed.

Without consulting each other, we both answered Sol's question with blank stares. And like some wordless act of sisterly togetherness, Linn moved to stand beside us and silently stared at him too.

Grandma always says that bullies are after a reaction, and when they don't get one, they're powerless. For sure, under the massed stares of the Love sisters, Sol looked just about ready to turn tail and leave, when some rotten thought slithered into his head. As the fledgling snegrin started sliming on to his face, he was looking at Linn. He was going to take another swipe at her nose (so to speak), I was sure of it. Specially since it had started to peel. . .

But someone stopped him in his weaselly tracks.

"Sol!" Ivy yelped at him, tugging at the bottom of his T-shirt to get his attention.

Sol frowned down, annoyed at being interrupted just as he was about to let some more venom fly.

"Why do you have a prawn on your head?" asked Ivy.

And sure enough, there it was, tucked into the spikes of his mini-fin haircut – a left-over from the tray of puff pastries that Rowan had chucked at him.

Sol instantly began slapping at his head, as if he was trying to dislodge a tarantula that had just dropped out of a tree. In a nanosecond, he'd disappeared off into the crowd of onlookers, who were probably wondering if the jerking, agitated teenage boy was on drugs or something. (No – he just had some unwanted seafood in his cool hairdo.)

"You were great!" I told Ivy, getting down on my knees to give her a bearhug.

"Well, done, Ives," said Linn, kissing the top of her head.

"Hee, hee!" giggled Ivy, unsure what all the fuss was about.

"Ah, I can't believe it!" Rowan cooed happily to herself, sneaking another peek at the photo on Billy's mobile. "I bought Alfie that toy bat at London zoo – I didn't know it meant *so* much to him!"

Linn suddenly made a barely audible retching sound.

So much for sisterly togetherness. . .

We hadn't even kissed yet, me and Billy, I realized, as I lay in the big tent (with Rowan, lots of luggage, three snoring dogs and a dried-out carnation in my fingers).

It had been a lovely, late-night, campfire tea here tonight, even if we were missing the fairy lights and crêpe paper garlands of last Saturday, when we'd first shipped up at Daniel's farm.

The reason it had been lovely – even though the food was a mismatch of whatever was left in our supplies – was that we were all together: Mum, Dad, five Love children, three dogs (plus a visiting

Arthur) and, the star turn, of course . . . Billy.

He'd made everyone laugh when he'd described leaving the note for his mum propped up behind the toaster, then had made himself some toast-to-go, not realizing that the heat would make the sheet of paper slowly curl and slither out of sight behind it. (The toaster, I mean, which is why Billy's parents didn't get his note and had gone doolally.)

And then he'd gotten serious and talked about phoning me back last night on the number he didn't recognize. . .

"I guessed it was that Sol guy as soon as he answered," Billy had explained. "But all I did was ask to speak to Ally."

"And?" I said, dread bursting in my chest. Whatever Sol had come out with *wasn't* going to be good. Whatever it was had been the last straw and made Billy get on the train to come find me. . .

"He told me you were hanging out with *him* now, and then he said –" Billy paused in his story and shot a glance at Tor and Ivy "– um, 'Bleep off, loser!'"

"OK, we get your drift, Billy!" Mum muttered hurriedly, in case Tor or Ivy suddenly worked out what rude-y word "bleep" stood for exactly.

Still, I was pretty glad that Mum had finally realized that lovely as Daniel was, his son wasn't particularly. She'd given me an extra big hug and squeeze when she and the kids and Linn finally headed sleepily up the hill to the farmhouse. . .

Next, it had been time for me and Rowan to slope off into the big tent, while Dad and Billy crawled yawning into the now-shabby-round-the-edges two-man tent.

Without even a kiss goodnight between me and Billy.

I twirled the dry stem of the carnation between my fingers, as the photos of Tor's pets on the wall started to get fuzzy, and sleep finally beckoned. . .

Whoooosh-whooosh. . .

Whoosh-whooosh. . .

Whooooooooosh-whooosh. . .

It wasn't just the whooshing that got my heart thundering like a road drill in my chest. It was the heavy breathing (sorry I didn't believe you, Tor), and the thudding and "oofing!!" going on outside too.

OK, so maybe the "oofing" didn't sound like a typical ghost thing to say. Which made me grab the pinky jam jar night-light I'd forgotten to blow out and stick my head warily out of the tent flap. . .

"Hello!" said a stupidly grinning Billy, rubbing his shin where it had just twanged into a guy rope.

"What are you doing?" I asked, crawling out on

to the grass, with my crimson jam jar held out in front of me. My gangly boy was wearing his shorts, T-shirt and ever-present baseball cap (did he sleep in that?).

This was the first time me and Billy had been alone since he'd shown up in St Ives. What deep and meaningful things would we end up saying to each other?

"I'm trying to find the loo."

Ah, romance. . .

"It's that way," I told him, holding the jam jar aloft and pointing to the big, dark hulk of the barn.

"Oh, cool. Wow, it's seriously dark out here, isn't it? I tripped over something *weird* just now, but I couldn't see what it was."

"Weird how?" I frowned up at him.

"Something by the side of your tent. Something soft. And moving. . ."

Urghh . . . I didn't like the sound of that. Were ghosts soft and moving?!

With a slightly shaky hand (and legs), I stood up and shone my jam jar light down the side of the tent, dreading what apparitions I might see. . .

"Arf!"

The "arf" came from a furry, black and white mound. At the sight and sound of me, Billy and the jam jar light, Arthur the elderly collie whoosh-whooshed his tail harder against the side of the tent, and panted in a breathy, old-time dog way.

"Tor's been thinking there was a ghost, but it's just Arthur," I mumbled, as everything became clear.

Yikes – Tor would be *mortified* in the morning, when he realized his "ghost" was actually an animal, and one he was big mates with.

As Arthur panted and whoosh-whooshed, joined by a sleepy, stretching posse of doggy friends, I blinked up at Billy, hovering in the half-light of the crimson jam jar I was holding.

And then my sweet, stupid boyfriend pulled a face, and came out with something that would have been pretty amazing if he hadn't said it in a dopey Patrick-the-sea-slug voice.

"By the way, I, uh, really . . . *y'know.*"

Wow.

If I wasn't very much mistaken, I think that was Billy Stevenson's adorably idiotic way of saying he *loved* me.

As I reeled at his (sort of) words, Billy immediately loped off in search of the shack-of-a-hut-of-a-loo.

And as he disappeared into the dark, with my

dogs (and Arthur) keeping him company, I realized I wanted to say something back.

"I really 'y'know' you too," I called out softly, "you big berk. . ."

Chapter 19

LOTS OF "Y'KNOW", ALLY...

Badda-bing, badda-bong, badda-badda-badda, bing, bing, bong!!

People passing were either laughing or tutting at us.

Badda-bing, badda-bong. Badda-badda-badda, bing, bing, bong!!

Where were we? Avebury, which happens to be in Wiltshire and is a very mystical place, with heaps of ancient ritualistic stones dotted around (yes, just like Stonehenge). Mum and Dad thought it was an amazing and educational place for us to stop, halfway through our journey (yes, just like Stonehenge).

Badda-bing, badda-bong, badda-badda-badda, bing, bing, bong!!

The car park at Avebury *isn't* so mystical, though. Specially this Saturday lunchtime in particular, with a fourteen-year-old boy sitting outside a minibus with "Sunshine Gospel Steel Band" splashed along the side, battering a bunch of up-turned saucepans with a wooden spoon and a stick with dog drool on it.

Badda-bing, badda-bong, badda-badda-badda, bing, bing, bong!!

"Billy," I said, trying to get his attention over the racket he was making. "*Billy!* Someone's going to ask us to leave!"

"Leave?" he grinned, enjoying hammering at his looky-likely steel drums. "How can you get asked to leave a car park?"

I gave a shrug. He was probably right, and I was probably worrying too much. I guess I'd spent so much of the previous week stressing that I'd got really good at it.

"Come on, Ally!" Billy tried to urge me into making a fool of myself. "Why don't you sing 'He's Got The Whole World In His Hands'? I'll drum along, and I *bet* people will start chucking money at us!"

Yeah, money or rotten fruit, maybe.

"Ally. . ." came a plaintive voice from inside the gospel bus. It was Tor, sticking his head out of a window, along with Rolf. "D'you think Mum and Dad and everyone will be back soon? 'Cause I think all the animals at home are really, *really* missing me now. . ."

I could see Tor's point. The stick insects were

probably devastated about being Tor-less for a week. I bet the goldfish had cried themselves to sleep in their tank every night. And I could just imagine Kevin the iguana being rigid with unhappiness (although he's generally rigid when he's hungry, bewildered and delirious too, so it's pretty hard to tell).

"I'm *sure* they'll be back soon," I nodded, although Mum, Dad, Linn, Ro and Ivy had only been gone fifteen minutes or so. They'd wanted us to come along and check out rocks too, but Tor was so gutted at having had to pat Arthur the ghost-dog bye-bye this morning that there was no *way* he wanted to leave the other dogs on their own in the gospel bus. Which meant of course that he couldn't be left on his own.

I'd gladly offered to stay behind, along with Billy. It's not that I had anything against ancient, ritualistic rocks . . . it's just that between Stonehenge, the Barbara Hepworth Museum and this place, I was just all stoned out. And I wanted time alone (ish) with Billy, since we'd both been a bit awkward with each other after using the "y'know" word last night. . .

"Hey, look, Tor – here come Linn and Ivy now!" said Billy, pointing his wooden spoon in the direction of my biggest and littlest sister, before doing a drumroll for them.

Which got Linn's eyes rolling.

"Billy, you can hear that racket from *miles* away!" she told him.

"Yeah?" said Billy, impressed with himself.

"I *like* it!" chirruped Ivy, taking off a welly and thumping it experimentally on the nearest pot.

"I didn't mean it as a compliment, Billy," Linn told him. "You should give it a rest, 'cause lots of people come her to meditate. I even saw two Buddhist monks wandering about just now!"

Buddhist monks? Rowan would *love* that, 'cause they wear those long, flowing, dark red robes. She'd be weaving between rocks towards them now, dying to tell them how to accessorize.

"Oh. Yeah. Sorry. . ." Billy started noisily picking up and putting away the pots and pans in the box marked "Kitchen Stuff".

"Aww. . ." muttered Ivy, disappointed.

"How come you came back so quickly?" I asked Linn.

"Ivy said she had a bruise in her tummy and needed a drink –"

Linn threw me a "yeah, *right!*" look.

"– but I think she just wanted to have a look at her new mug again."

Ah, the "Ivy from St Ives" mug . . . now that there weren't a zillion people staring and saying

"Awwww" at her, our kid sis had got very excited about seeing a weeny version of herself. She'd be even *more* excited if she knew there was a whole *box* of mugs with mini-Ivys packed in the back of the van (one for each member of the family, plus Grandma and Stanley).

Bleep!

Doo, doo, dee, doopy-doo, doo, doo dooooo. . .

The bleep! came from Billy's phone; the blast of Beyonce's "Crazy In Love" was from Linn's (perfect for any passing meditating monks, I'm sure, Linn!).

"Gee, that's *nice!*" Billy said sarcastically, gazing at some photo image on his mobile. "Do you think that's Sol's way of saying 'it's been great knowing you'?"

I took a look and then immediately wished I hadn't. Let's just say I wasn't looking a weaselly face – it was a whole *different* pair of cheeks. . .

"Do you miss Sol, then, Ally?" grinned Billy.

"About as much as the shack-of-a-hut-of-a-loo. . ." I mumbled in reply.

"Miss you already, Sol!" said Billy, in his dopey cartoon voice, as he firmly hit the delete button.

"*That's* my slug!" I laughed, giving him the thumbs-up.

Billy's face fell.

"Why do you keep calling me a slug, Ally?"

Uh-oh. I'd only got the happy/stupid Billy back again; I didn't want him to go all sensitive/confused on me again.

"It's only 'cause of that *Squarebob Spongepants* voice you've been doing!"

Billy frowned at me from under his baseball cap. "What, Patrick the Starfish?"

OK, maybe Billy wasn't the *only* stupid one in our relationship. Maybe I needed to pay more attention in biology, so I could tell the difference between a sea slug and a starfish. Or maybe I just needed to watch more dumb cartoons with him. . .

"Hey, what's wrong with *her*?"

I hadn't realized Rowan had joined us.

"Where're Mum and Dad?" I asked her, ignoring her question.

"They're all loved up and smoochy – I thought I'd leave them to it," she smiled. "But what's up with Linn?"

Last Saturday, Linn had spent most of the journey to Cornwall with her forehead pressed to the window of the gospel bus in total misery. She was doing it again now, only she was on the outside this time.

"Linn?" I said, stepping towards her, and spotting the mobile clenched in one dangling hand.

My heart skipped a beat or three when Linn turned to look at me. It wasn't because of the smudge of dust and dirt where her forehead had been pressed against the side of the bus; it was because I saw that she'd been crying. Had she had terrible news? Had she just found out that Mum and Dad had booked another family holiday or something?

"Is she sick?" asked Tor, leaning further out of the gospel bus window in alarm. Rolf leant out too, in case anyone was talking about sausages.

Before we could reassure Tor, Linn did the most un-Linn-like thing in the history of Linn . . . she tilted her head back, and at the top of her voice shouted: "I'M GOING TO *EDINBURGH*!!!" (Cue meditating Buddhist monks toppling over in alarm.)

"You got your exam results?" I said, asking yet another of my many dumb questions.

Linn nodded, tears spilling (messily) from her eyes.

"Uh-huh. Grandma just called – she's round at ours feeding the pets and saw the envelope with my results. So I got her to open it and read them out to me. And I got all As and one B!"

"Oh, congratulations, Linn!" said Rowan, smiling and now crying too, as she went to hug our big sis.

"We're going to *miss* you!"

OK, so that's when I got a bit wibbly too; when it suddenly sunk in that in just a few weeks, the Grouch Queen would be gone. I think I needed to join in this sisterly cuddle. . .

As we three oldest Love children wrapped our arms around each other, I was only vaguely aware of the tugging at my T-shirt. But I certainly felt the tap of a wellie on my shin.

"You doing *happy* crying?" asked Ivy, gazing up at us all.

"Absolutely!" I smiled, scooping her up to join in this group hug.

Now that we were going to lose one member of the family, this special little sister – grown in St Ives – would be even *more* special. With her pinkness and cuteness, she'd keep us all so busy it would help us not miss Linn (quite so much). . .

"Hey, Ally," I heard Billy say, close by me.

Passing a wriggling Ivy over to Linn, I turned to see what Billy wanted – and found myself in the middle of our first kiss since he'd turned up yesterday.

It was a very nice kiss.

It made me go a bit wibbly in the middle.

How romantic.

Except for that tiny clicking noise.

"Huh?" I huh'ed, breaking away and finding myself caught on camera (phone). "What are you doing?"

Billy brought his extended arm in closer, pressed a couple of keys.

"Just thought I'd send Sol something to remember us by," he grinned.

I guess zapping a picture of a kiss was a lot nicer than mooning back, and if it made Billy feel like he'd got the last word, then fine.

As for me, I suddenly decided that I just wanted to get all chilled out like a Buddhist monk, and meditate on the good stuff that had come out of our holiday.

And those just happened to be. . .

- A very nice box of mugs.
- A small sister who'll be famous (or at least in the kitchen cupboards of St Ives tourists for ever more).
- A new mate for Linn (she'd spent most of the drive to Avebury texting Lana).
- And of course (and most importantly) me, Dad and Rowan found out that the people we loved all loved us *right* back. Which was very cool indeed (y'know!).

"Hey!" I heard Dad's voice call out, as he and Mum strolled towards us, hand-in-hand. "Is the gospel steel band ready to go home?"

Hallelujah – we sure were. . .

We've been back from holiday for a whole three days now, Grandma, and those are all my ramblings. They might have made you feel a bit dizzy, but then remember, that could be 'cause your sinuses are all blocked up too.

Must go . . . I've just realized the time: there are only five weeks and four days till Linn leaves for Edinburgh, so I'd better round up the kids and the pets and go bug her, since she'll miss our noise, mess, and shed fur so much when she's gone. . .

Lots of "y'know" *,

Ally :c) **

(your Grandchild No. 3)

* Ha!

** That's a smiley face, by the way. Though with those asterixes, it looks like a smiley face with two warts on its chin.

PS Winslet and Ben are sniffing at the wardrobe

door. I think it's jammed, and that knocking sound is Tor trying to let me know he's stuck in there.

PPS I'm rambling again, aren't I? Sorry. . .

KaReN McCoMBiE

"A funny and talented author"
Books Magazine

Once upon a time (OK, 1990), Karen McCombie jumped in her beat-up car with her boyfriend and a very bad-tempered cat, leaving her native Scotland behind for the bright lights of London and a desk at "J17" magazine. She's lived in London and acted like a teenager ever since.

The fiction bug bit after writing short stories for "Sugar" magazine. Next came a flurry of teen novels, and of course the best-selling "Ally's World" series, set around and named after Alexandra Palace in North London, close to where Karen lives with her husband Tom, little daughter Milly and an assortment of cats.

PS If you want to know more about Karen check out her website at <u>karenmccombie.com</u>. Karen says, "It's sheeny and shiny, furry and, er, funny (in places)! It's everything you could want from a website and a weeny bit more…"

PPS Email us for a **Karen's Club** newsletter at <u>publicity@scholastic.co.uk</u> and keep in touch with Karen!

ALLY'S WORLD

Hi,
There's lots going on in my
world – here's just some of
what I have to deal with!!

3 SISTERS – 1 BOSSY,
1 BONKERS, 1 VERY PINK

1 SPACE-Cadet BROTHER

1 dad

1 MUM

1 SCRUFFY HOUSE iN a NiCE PLACE
with a FUNNY NAME

1 GREAT VIEW FROM MY bedROOM

2 dOGS – WINSLET aNd ROLF
(dON't EVEN ask)

~~5 cats~~ – 1's CaLLED COLiN

Oh, aNd FRiENds – LOts.

Now that you've finished this story, get into one
of my other adventures – there's heaps to
choose from.

"Once you start reading you can't stop" *Mizz*

To: You
From: Stella
Subject: Stuff

Hi,

You'd think it would be cool to live by the sea with all that sun, sand and ice cream. But, believe me, it's not such a breeze. I miss my best mate Frankie, my terror twin brothers drive me nuts and my mum and dad have gone daft over the country dump, sorry, "character cottage", that we're living in. I'm bored, and I'm fed up with being the new girl on the block.
Hey! Maybe if we hang out together we could have some fun here. Whadya think?
Catch up with me in the rest of the *Stella Etc.* series.
I bet we'll have loads to talk about.
CU soon.
LOL

stella
XXX

PS Here's a pic of me on a bad hair day (any day actually) with my mate Frankie. I'm the one on the right!

"Super-sweet and cool as an ice cream" *Mizz*

OUT NOW!

Marshmallow Magic and the Wild Rose Rouge

An extract…

1

Shhh . . .

Hello.

My name's Lemmie.

Do you want to know a secret?

The secret is, I've got *lots* of secrets.

Some of my secrets are so old I've kind of half-forgotten them.

Some are around me all the time, every day.

Some are so weird I can't tell anyone about them, 'cause they'd laugh at me or think I was a freak. (Well, drawing circles around the freckles on your arms when you're sleepwalking *is* pretty freaky, I guess.)

Some of my secrets are so spangly and special that I hold them inside of me, like a sparkler in the dark.

My secrets come in all shapes and sizes: some are

weeny and floaty-light; some are heart-shaped, and some are, er . . . mouse-shaped.

One secret in particular's so *humungously* big, I can't even bring myself to think about it, never mind write it down. . .

But then some of my secrets can be amazingly, dazzlingly *ordinary* too. Like with Dad, I could *never* tell him that his hip Liam Gallagher haircut looks less hip and more like a deranged farmer's attacked him with a pair of sheep shears. That chunklet of truth would be *way* too cruel.

And with Mum, I can't exactly let her know that the "cute" knock-knock thing we do when she comes to my bedroom door is just something I invented to give me time to hide any stray marshmallow magic under the bed.

Speaking of Mum and Dad, they know a couple of my secrets, but not all of them.

My best friends Morven and Jade, they know some of the marshmallow magic, but that's about it.

There's only one person who knows everything about *everything*, and that's Rose Rouge (of course).

Oh, and before I forget, here's another secret: Lemmie's not my real name.

Confused yet?

Hey, welcome to the club – I manage to confuse myself *all* the time. . .